# THE
# *Tatterbitty*

GEORGE S. HAINES

authorHOUSE®

AuthorHouse™
1663 Liberty Drive
Bloomington, IN 47403
www.authorhouse.com
Phone: 1 (800) 839-8640

Published by AuthorHouse  02/22/2019

ISBN: 978-1-5462-7969-3 (sc)
ISBN: 978-1-5462-7967-9 (hc)
ISBN: 978-1-5462-7968-6 (e)

Library of Congress Control Number: 2019901521

Print information available on the last page.

PREVIOUS MYSTERY ADVENTURES
BY
GEORGE S. HAINES

\*\*\*\*\*\*\*\*\*\*\*\*\*\*\*\*

The Giant Horseshoe Mystery
\*\*\*\*\*

THE X Y Z Mystery
\*\*\*\*\*

The Red Pick-Up Truck Mystery
\*\*\*\*\*

The Professor with Many Faces
\*\*\*\*\*

The Wreck of the 'Cincy' Queen
\*\*\*\*\*

The King Bee
\*\*\*\*\*

The Legend of the Bent Organ Pipes
\*\*\*\*\*

Intrigue at 404 Appalling Street

# To All Readers

CONTINUING WITH THE ABSORBING AND captivating adventures of detectives Sam and Howie, this mystery will keep you involved until you read the surprising conclusion. New characters keep emerging to complicate the intriguing scene as the detectives assist Sheriff Neverfine and Inspector Snooper in pursuing nefarious law breakers.

Lacking objectionable language this novel is appropriate for all ages. My prayer is for this inspiring story to honor the teachings of Jesus Christ and continue to enhance the glory of God.

Many individuals contributed suggestions and enhancements as the story transpired. Thanks to Myra Jane, my wife, for her patient reading of the manuscript and offering succinct suggestions.

And, words are not adequate to describe the artistic talents of Betty Wedeles, the artist who created the tantalizing visual impression of THE TATTERBITTY for the cover of this mystery.

# *A Prologue*

I T SEEMS INTRIGUE AND FURTIVE actions continue to occur in and
around the mansion located at 404 Appalling Street in Marston,
Indiana, a thriving city that is home to thousands of ambitious
residents and the address of many prospering industries. This
mansion, a unique dwelling, built during the early 1900's by Ovid
and Samantha Prudely, served as their resident for many years. Many
local residents consider the mansion to be a distinctive landmark.

The fertile farm land surrounding Marston supplied a bounty of
agricultural products for the Allied armed forces during the recent
war. Now in the year 1948 local residents have settled into peaceful
post-war activities. Every local citizen assumes that the war-time
efforts are fading memories. Peaceful endeavors now consume their
thinking and activities.

However, Gerhard and Horst, two night-time employees at the
local Millsaap Flour Mill find themselves stuck in the area as illegal
German immigrants. They are not participating in the post-war
enthusiasm. They face the reality that their long-time mentor, Red
Fox, is dead. Now they must survive without his constant directives
and monetary support. As illegal residents their constant objective

is to obtain the necessary funds to finance their return to Bavaria, their homeland.

Complicating their troubled lives and uncertain future, Mrs. Gertrude Everlite, neighbor to the Prudely mansion, recalls visions that occurred during the war years. She remembers seeing flashing lights emanating from the Prudely mansion's tower. She relates these suppressed memories to Sheriff Neverfine. Detectives Sam and Howie are called to action, ordered by the sheriff to investigate the reported occurrences of strange lights coming from the tower during the recent conflict.

What will their inquiry reveal? Did the lights serve to transmit covert and strategic information? Perhaps the flashing lights conveyed secret and clandestine messages. If so, who sent the information and for what purposes? And, since the observation of the lights by Mrs. Everlite occurred during the war, is this information important now in the year 1948?

You, the reader, have become an accessory to these weird happenings because the situation just described has piqued your interest and imagination. Already you have formed opinions as to the reason for and the objectives of the flashing lights. Now, read on to determine if any of your preconceived explanations are correct.

Following is a roster of places and participants keeping you oriented as you follow the script of this thrilling mystery:

## THE TATTERBITTY

| | |
|---|---|
| Sheriff Byron Neverfine | long time chief lawman of Gurant County. |
| Never Drip Coffee Shop | popular eatery in Marston. |
| Hortense | waitress at The Never Drip Coffee Shop. |
| Inspector Snooper | Hershel 'Snooper' Sneupenhauger, second in command at Sheriff Neverfine's jail office. |
| Mrs. Gertrude Everlite | next door neighbor to the Prudely mansion. |
| Mr. Pudgmor | Inspector Snooper's instructor at his self defense class. |
| Ovid and Samantha Prudely | prior owners of the mansion at 404 Appalling Street. |
| Belvedear Everlite | husband of Gertrude Everlite. |
| Colonel Helmut Schmidt (Red Fox) | former Nazi Panzer tank commander. Director of espionage in Indiana. |
| Ernesto | cook at The Never Drip Coffee Shop. |

Dr. Stephen Younger ............................... pediatrician at Younger Children's Hospital.

Rev. Rob Kneel ...................................... distinguished pastor of The Marston Methodist Church.

Admiral Theodore Radar ....................... U. S. naval officer.

Zsofia .................................................... cook at Marston County jail.

Gladys Fedders ...................................... neighbor of the Prudely's.

Jane Olive Prudely ................................ daughter of Ovid and Samantha.

Joseph Ashley Prudely ........................... son of Ovid and Samantha.

Dr. T. Boner ........................................... physician assigned to the jail.

Captain Morsely ..................................... Marston policeman.

Mary Nupulse ........................................ nurse at Marston Hospital.

# Chapter 1

S HERIFF BYRON NEVERFINE APPROACHED THE Never Drip Coffee Shop with steps of determination. Yawning he glanced at the image of his rather ample physique reflected by the single, clouded glass panel located in the sagging yellow entrance door. He stopped, expanded his chest, adjusted his tan tie and pulled up his matching trousers.

Frowning at the necessity of loosening his belt another notch he made a silent vow to consume fewer doughnuts each day and add only two spoonfuls of sugar to each of his mugs of coffee.

Entering the diner he straightened his shoulders and narrowed his eyelids. Following his usual custom he scanned the faces of all customers enjoying the usual hunger-reducing breakfast offerings. He glanced at the 1948 calendar hanging on the wall next to the kitchen door. A few dates in October had already been marked off with large X's.

The coffee shop, a weather-beaten landmark located on Adams Street in Marston, Indiana, near the county courthouse, opened Monday thru Saturday at 5 a.m. The eatery closed at night only when the last customer sauntered out the door, usually burping loudly.

Immediately the tantalizing odors released by the frying bacon and brewing coffee enveloped the sheriff. He inhaled deeply allowing the tantalizing aromas to further enhance his appetite and expand his commanding physique. He greeted Hortense, the long-time gracious server, with a smile. Quickly she guided him to a back corner booth, his favorite spot for furtive conversations.

A few minutes later Inspector Hershel Sneupenhauger, commonly known by all his acquaintances as Snooper, eased his way through the same door. Spotting the sheriff he moped along with a slouch and joined the county's chief law officer at the rear booth.

Hortense approached the lawmen and set two coffee mugs on the table top with dull thuds. Smiling she filled the cracked and smudged mugs to the brim and said, "Welcome, Sheriff and Snooper. Do you both want the usual fare this morning?"

"Yes, thank you, Hortense," replied the sheriff before Snooper had a chance to respond. "And, bring four of your signature donuts, the large ones with the chocolate icing on top, er-r on second thought make that two doughnuts."

Snooper looked around at the boisterous customers who were chomping loudly, slurping coffee, talking and gesturing emphatically at the same time. Relieved that none of the early morning 'regulars' were looking in his direction he faced the sheriff and inquired, "Why the sudden and urgent request to meet me here at the Never Drip Coffee Shop so early on this Monday morning? We usually enjoy signature morning coffee in your office at the jail."

"Snooper," replied the sheriff with a solemn demeanor as he leaned forward and engaged the inspector with serious eye contact,

"I wanted to privately discuss with you an item that will be on our agenda this Wednesday, October 13...mark your calendar.... when we meet with the members of my 'jail cabinet' made up of the usual law-enforcement and support folks."

The sheriff stopped abruptly, pointed and asked, "By the way, how did you get that black eye? Your face looks like my neighbor's dog, a Dalmatian."

"Never mind the eye....What development is so important that we need to call for a special cabinet meeting this Wednesday? And why did you ask me to join you here at this coffee shop so early for breakfast this morning?"

The sheriff scooted forward on the wood bench seat. Glancing around to make sure their discussion remained private he looked intently at Snooper and quietly said, "Mrs. Gertrude Everlite crept into my office last Friday morning and sat down before I could greet her by offering a cup of coffee. She sat on the edge of her chair massaging and twisting her worn, patched money bag. She seemed quite upset and nervous."

"You must be referring to the widow who lives next door on the east side of the Ovid Prudely mansion. I remember we thought at one time she had colluded with Ovid to cause the death of Belvadear, her husband."

"Yes, that's the right person. After a few minutes of quiet fidgeting and hand-wringing she opened up and we talked for at least an hour."

"Did she seem to be relieved that the scoundrel, Red Fox, is now dead? Does she remember he utilized the underground chemical laboratory located beneath the Prudely carriage house to produce unusual and possibly illegal products and compounds? After all, that activity occurred next door to her property."

"Yes, on both counts. Indeed she smiled as we discussed the demise of Red Fox. Mrs. Everlite also complimented you, Snooper, for your courageous actions in confronting, subduing and arresting Bruno, his patsy, during our successful raid at the mansion when we arrested Red Fox."

"That undercover action you spearheaded at the Prudely house certainly proved to be a significant event," smiled Snooper, straightening his posture in the booth. "But, what concern motivated Mrs. Everlite to venture out of her house and come to your office without an invitation?"

At that point Hortense appeared with a coffee pot in one hand and their bill in the other hand. "Would you two gentlemen like your coffee mugs refilled?"

"No thank you, Hortense. And, tell Ernesto, the cook, that he fixed the scrambled eggs and grilled the bacon to just the right taste."

Hortense smiled and left their booth to meet other customers. The sheriff burped and wiped his lips vigorously several times with wrinkled tan paper napkins. He cleared his throat, bent his large frame forward, looked directly at the inspector and whispered, "Mrs. Everlite locked her eyes on mine and said she wanted to share what she considered disturbing incidents that happened months ago. She seemed burdened to relate her observations of night-time occurrences in the Prudely mansion that seemed weird to her, almost bizarre and freakish."

4

"Be more specific, Sheriff," requested Snooper, scooting forward and frowning slightly. "Did these events occur during the same periods as our surveillance of the activities in and about the Prudely property, the case we dubbed, *'Intrigue at 404 Appalling Street' ?"*

"Yes, she vividly remembers those incidents. But the reason she ventured out of her house and came to my office last Friday is her recollection of strange happenings at the Prudely mansion during prior years."

After slurping more coffee the sheriff continued. "Gertrude related that during nighttime hours on several occasions during 1943 and 1944 she observed flickering lights that seemed to originate inside the rectangular windows located at the top of the tower."

"Are you referring to the silo-like formation that is part of the Prudely house on the northeast corner?" asked Snooper, forking another long slice of grilled bacon into his wide-open mouth.

"Yes, several of the Prudely's neighbors have offered comments about that part of the structure. Local builders and architects have said that type of design seemed to be a rather common feature for Victorian-style homes built during the late 1800's and early 1900's."

"Did she see these flashing lights often?"

"Yes, Gertrude said the lights began to appear after the remodeling of the mansion and often during the war years, especially during 1944."

"Why did Mrs. Everlite come to your office and report these sightings now, in October, 1948, three years after the end of the

Second World War? Did the news of the death of Red Fox encourage her to discuss the intermittent lights with you?"

"I asked her the same questions. She replied that the focal point of her attention and efforts during those earlier stressful months focused on her son, Dexter. She reminded me that her next-door neighbor, Ovid Prudely, as an experiment had applied a chemical substance to Dexter's face giving his skin a greenish-yellow hue. Later, in the same laboratory under the Prudely carriage house, Red Fox devised a chemical substance that restored Dexter's face to the normal color. During those intervening, nerve-wracking weeks she dismissed the sightings of lights flashing from the mansion tower as less important than her son's anguish about his skin condition."

Reaching for and lifting his coffee cup the sheriff burped, sipped and swallowed loudly. He leaned forward and looked firmly at Snooper. "Recently, she recalled the series of flickering lights and thought they might be important. She decided to come to my office to report her sightings."

Snooper remained silent with a thoughtful countenance, staring at his coffee mug.

The sheriff continued, "She seemed rather embarrassed to relate to me her observations that occurred so many months ago," added the sheriff.

"Toward the end of the conference she became quiet, gazing at the wall in my office. After a few seconds of thought she expressed doubts as to whether the lights represented anything important. She said her conscience is now clear since she related the events to me."

Pointing his finger at Snooper he stated, "Now, Inspector, as law enforcement officers we need to decide if personnel available at this sheriff's office should probe further into this phenomenon of flashing lights during past years or drop the matter as now unimportant."

"What do you think?" asked Snooper. "Should we initiate an investigation based on this new information, Sheriff?"

"I will present the gist of my conversation with Mrs. Everlite at our cabinet meeting this Wednesday afternoon in the jail conference room. I will invite detectives Sam and Howie to join us and Captain Firmly, representing the Indiana State Police. Also, Spade Digger, our mortician, should meet with us since he thinks he is part of our group."

"That sounds like the professional approach. We'll let the cabinet members decide the next steps to take. I would predict they will suggest we forget about your recent conversation with Mrs. Everlite. The information she presented is past history. We need to focus on recent crimes disturbing the residents in Marston."

"You are probably right, Inspector. We need to utilize our time and efforts responding to the current concerns of our citizens. Therefore, since detectives Sam Hames and Howie Newbald are not officially members of the sheriff's office personnel, I may ask them to pursue this matter and report back to the cabinet at a later date."

"That's a good idea, Sheriff. They know all about the Prudely property and the recent 'shenanigans' that occurred at that location. Howie and Sam assisted our department personnel in the capture of Red Fox and his two 'patsies', Bruno and Udo.....Yes, the two detectives are the logical persons to continue this investigation....

if the cabinet members so decide." The inspector relaxed, grateful the burden of investigating the blinking lights would not be his responsibility.

The two lawmen scooted out from their seats at the booth. As they walked toward the hostess counter to pay their bill, the sheriff stopped, pointed at Snooper's left eye and inquired, "Snoop, that black eye makes the entire side of your face look terrible. Did you run into the bathroom door?"

The inspector remained mute until they emerged from the eatery. Hesitating he leaned forward and looked carefully at his reflection in the front window of the diner. Turning quickly he moved forward at a faster pace.

After a few more steps he replied softly, "Sheriff, a few weeks ago I enrolled in a self-defense class. Mr. Pudgmor, the instructor, teaches us a technique he labels 'aggressive jousting'."

"Really? Tell me more, Snoop. Since your class members are not knights riding horses, how do you joust?"

"He begins each class day by demonstrating the craft of defensive fighting using agile foot work and forceful sparring, sort of like what I call 'cock-fighting'."

"Snooper, where did you learn anything about 'cock fighting'?"

"Err, no place. I never witnessed any cock-fighting. My former neighbors told me about the 'sport' held weekly out in the country in an old barn."

"What does all this talk have to do with your black eye?"

"After Pudgmor's forceful demonstration we put on the boxing gloves. He pairs up the students and we practice jousts. Yesterday my opponent caught me off guard and popped me real good on the left side of my face."

"That's wonderful, Snooper. You definitely need to enhance your skills in the area of self-defense. Describe the makeup of your group. How old is your student-opponent at the jousting class?"

"The class includes male and female students of all ages."

"You evaded my question. How old is the student who 'popped you' in the eye?"

"She is one of the younger participants."

"Snoop, how old is your jousting partner?"

"Errrr, I would judge my sparring partner is about ten years old. She is quite mature and agile for her age. Dancing around and bobbing up and down she does not present a good target for my well-aimed jousts."

"So is she quite aggressive?" inquired the sheriff, smiling widely.

"During our session yesterday she sidestepped, feigned a left jab and with a fast right hook she 'knuckled' me smack-dab on my left eye. She, of course, apologized as she helped me up from the mat."

The sheriff, smiling widely, walked briskly in the bright sunshine toward the jail. The Inspector, dour-faced, slouched along a few steps behind holding his hand over his left eye hoping not to meet anyone. Quickly the assumed importance of Mrs. Everlite's recent conversation with the sheriff regarding the flickering lights evaporated into the pleasant October air.

# Chapter 2

GERHARD, BLEARY-EYED AND YAWNING WIDELY squinted at Horst, his working companion on the night shift at The Millsaap Flour Mill. He reached over and thumped Horst soundly on the chest. The shorter German national lying prone, his head resting upon a sack of flour, wriggled and jerked awake. He bolted upright and crouched forward with clenched fists.

"Calm down, Horst. Sit back down on that sack of flour and listen to me," blared Gerhard emphatically as he leaned forward. "I've been sitting here awake during the two 30-minute breaks from our work at the mill thinking for both of us. We must find a way to get out of this foreign town and return to our beloved homeland and soon."

"I agree, Gerhard," sighed his co-worker with resignation and fatigue in his voice."We've been working undercover for months toting bags of flour from the mill to the storage shed, then later to the buyers' trucks. My hair is white and I breathe this awful white flour dust twelve hours every night."

"And," added Horst, "since I read in that local newspaper I salvaged from the garbage bin about the unfortunate death of Colonel

Helmut Schmidt, our patron and boss, we are now in a hopeless and dead-end employment without a sponsor and confidant."

"Yeah, as long as the colonel, Red Fox to us, remained active here in Marston he gave us our orders and insisted we remain in this back-breaking job. We did all of the colonel's unpleasant chores."

"However, Gerhard, our employment here at the Millsaap Flour Mill has served as a welcome cover for our real purpose in this town, the sabotage of local industry."

"Well, Red Fox stupidly fell in his jail cell at the county lock-up when that dopey Inspector Snooper served him a meal of goulash. Snooper slipped on the floor and the Hungarian goulash splashed into Red Fox's face and mouth. He choked, collapsed on the concrete floor and cracked his head wide open. At least that's the story reported in *The Marston Tribune,* the local newspaper. He can no longer offer us financial help, Horst. We will survive now by our own efforts and gut-instinct."

"You are absolutely right. Red Fox as our patron told us what to do here in Marston to help the Fuhrer's cause. But we have brains too, Gerhard. We can survive and perhaps profit without the Colonel's constant guidance."

"What do you mean profit, Horst? We earn only a few American dollars per week at this mill moving sacks of flour from one place to another plus keeping this building respectable."

"Wait a minute, Gerhard. I just remembered something. A light bulb has just been turned on again in my brain. I know a way we can escape from this town and return to Germany. I'll share my thoughts with you later."

"No one here at the Millsaap Flour Mill has ever suspected we worked with Red Fox and helped him with his espionage duties, especially when he tried to blow up the Jumper Parachute Factory out at the west end of town a few years ago."

"Yeah, I'll have to admit Red Fox learned well his devious skills at espionage. He proved to be an expert undercover agent. His plan to destroy the local parachute factory almost succeeded, with our help of course."

"As I recall, Horst, those two pesky detectives, Sam and Howie, I don't know their last names, discovered our plotting and our plan failed at the last moment."

"For a long time I thought they served as deputies working for the blustery Sheriff Neverfine," added Gerhard. "I didn't know the detectives had their own agency located across the street from the jailhouse."

"Rehashing old news, Gerhard, certainly isn't going to help us to vacate this mill, leave Marston and get back to Germany."

"I know, Horst. We are in a serious predicament with very limited resources and we lack the legal documents necessary for our travel to Germany. We don't have Red Fox to direct our lives or sustain us with money. The passports he obtained for us illegally a few years ago ended up in a bag of flour sent to some western state, due to your stupidity."

"Gerhard, if I concentrate and think real hard a solution to our situation will come to my active mind. Yes, let me tell you about my latest brainstorm. I believe we can combine our talents and leave this city of Marston and be on the way to our homeland."

"You haven't had an original idea in years, Horst. What makes you think your pea-sized brain has generated a plan to secretly and miraculously transfer our bodies from this flour mill to Bavaria?"

"Well, I, we can be proud that our efforts helped Red Fox with his secret undercover plans here in Marston. The plan that Red Fox devised to destroy the parachute factory out at the west end of town proved to be our most proud achievement."

"I agree, Horst; that facility fabricated 500 parachutes for United States airmen every week."

"That year, 1944, proved to be our most exciting and productive period of espionage, Gerhard."

"Yah, we sure made a lot of trips up and down the three levels in this building using the hoist and then climbing the steps to the cupola at the top of this mill."

"From that vantage point the entire city of Marston became our domain as we could see the entire town in all directions especially during moonlit nights."

"That's right, Horst...we had a beautiful vantage spot especially during the black-outs in 1943 and '44."

"Also, Horst, your knowledge of the Morse Code and the two years of your patriotic service on German U-Boats gave you valuable experience," added Gerhard. "You acquired an indispensable ability to send and interpret signals using flashing lights generated by us and our colleagues from the tower at the Prudely mansion."

"I'll have to admit, Gerhard, the months of 1944 gave me a euphoria of importance as we demonstrated our faithful adherence to the Fuhrer and the Nazi cause."

"I agree. And when our plan to destroy the parachute factory in 1944 failed, I felt my life-long journey as a devoted Nazi had come to an abrupt end....Suddenly I felt defeated and useless as a German spy."

"Our mission here in Marston, Indiana, is now at an end. We cease to have any reason to remain here since the war is over and our mentor, Red Fox, is dead."

"Horst, we are vagabond Nazis. We would be hated by the other workers here at the mill and the local populace of Marston if the people knew our true identity. They would tie us up and throw our worthless corpses in the same river water that powers this flour mill."

"Yah, we must vacate this town soon and use every skill, trick and maneuver taught to us by Red Fox to accomplish our exit....We will use every means, legal or not, to find a way to return to our home."

Gerhard shifted his position sitting on the sacks of flour and faced his co-worker. "Now, Horst, I would like to hear more about this brilliant idea you referred to a few minutes ago, something about a plan to leave this town and return to Germany."

"Here is my brainstorm, my strategy for our escape from Marston." Horst moved closer to his companion and asked, "Do you remember Klaus Egglebest, a fellow student when we completed anatomy classes and laboratories at the Hostead Optical Laboratory in Germany?"

"Yah, I recall that nerdy, 'prima-donna'. Why do you bring up his name now?"

"I wonder if Klaus, now an optics scientist and German undercover agent, is still employed out on Adams Street at The Marston Optical Company."

"Is Klaus the invisible spy who managed to furnish Germany with high priority periscope lenses for our German U-Boats a few years ago, Horst?"

"Yah, his secret espionage work here in Marston helped to supply Germany with the necessary lenses after the nasty Royal Air Force bombers leveled our optics factory in Germany."

"As I recall every student in our classes at Hostead hated Klaus. He always appeared pompous and dressed in nerdy-looking clothes. He sneaked around and copied our lecture notes at the end of every optics class in Berlin," replied Gerhard.

"I remember him. He walked around with his chest puffed out and he always assumed a superior attitude. He alienated all his classmates. I'll bet that's the reason he ended up in this country as a secret agent," added Horst.

"Yah, his superiors probably wanted to be rid of him. But how can he help us now, Horst? The war 's been over for three years."

"Klaus is one of two or three persons who transmitted messages to us here at this mill by using flashing lights from the Prudely tower. Red Fox, as you may recall, also used the signal lamp from that location to send many of the messages. Then a self-described young girl appeared out of nowhere and sent several signals to us."

"You mean the lass who shared with us her description of her outlandish dresses she wore made of colorful cloth strips?"

"Yah, she acted like we, as her brothers in communication, would like to know about her rather distinct attire."

"Red Fox also coerced a dwarf recluse living as a hermit in the tower to send signals. And, if you will remember, Klaus Egglebest himself frequently sent us specific messages with directions—such as the number of periscope lenses and the date he would bring them here so we could place them in the sacks of flour and send them on to the next stop."

"Yah, Gerhard, I fondly remember those days. Klaus would bring us the necessary number of lenses by locking them in a secure bag and walking on back streets from the Holstead Optical Laboratory to the Mississinewa river. He rowed a small boat along the shore of the river at night to The Millsaap Flour Mill."

"Yah, we would meet him," continued Horst, standing up and waving his arms about, "follow his directions and place the lenses in the bags of flour we marked with black paint to alter the **M** letters to make them more bold and easy to spot. Those bags of flour, along with others, would be loaded in the same rowboat, taken to the Prudely mansion and placed in the tower ready for the next segment of the long journey to Germany."

"Horst, don't you feel sorry for poor, pompous Klaus? He had to lug those bags of flour with the lenses hidden inside from the Mississinewa River bank through those dark, back alleys to the Prudely mansion."

"How did Klaus unlock the door to access the tower so easily at night to deliver the marked bags of flour? He also needed to enter the tower to send and receive messages by Morse Code and, to stow the bags of flour with the lenses inside."

"He said he found a way to gain entrance to the tower at night.... something about a bear's nose."

"A bear's nose! Now I know Klaus is daft, Gerhard."

"Crazy or not, Klaus could communicate with us by using the signal lamp up in the tower of the Prudely mansion."

"Yah, those heady, intoxicating nights when we helped to secretly move the periscope lenses from this flour mill to the Prudely tower gave me a reason to proudly puff out my chest."

"I had the same euphoric feelings, Horst. Then, if you will remember, a 'borrowed' Jiffy Cola delivery truck transported the bags of flour marked with the bold letter **M** from the Prudely tower to Chicago. At the river the marked sacks of flour would be loaded at night on to a small power boat that navigated Lake Michigan and the St. Lawrence Seaway all the way east to Halifax."

"Yah, at that location our German agents removed the lenses from the marked flour sacks and hid them inside watermelons purchased at the Halifax fruit and vegetable market. From there the lenses traveled inside the melons by fishing trawler to the waters surrounding Iceland."

"Then finally," continued Horst, "the melons with the lenses inside were off-loaded to submarines for the under-water journey to Germany where the lenses found a place in the periscopes of our submarines."

"We have pleasure remembering those nights, Horst."

"But how will Klaus know we are now desperate to leave this town?"

"Klaus brags he is an expert craftsman in the area of producing glass lenses for cameras, telescopes, binoculars and all types of scopes. He perfected the art of making optical glass, free from bubbles and other flaws. Ordinary layman like us think the process is so simple. But Klaas said it consisted of the highest degree of manufacturing skill and control. The resultant glass has to be free of iron and bubbles; also, colorless and completely transparent."

"I'm listening, Horst. I know all about his capabilities in the area of optics but how can he help us get back to Germany?"

"We will ask Klaus to facilitate our exit from this town and country."

"But how can Klaus expedite our trip from this flour mill to our lovely Bavaria?"

"He will use his usual pompous, self-assured demeanor and give the necessary orders to his subordinates."

Horst paused, then said, "Remember, Gerhard, he has a superior position and is a trusted research manager at the optical lab. He will be able to acquire passports and airplane tickets for the three of us, probably at the optical laboratory's expense."

"Horst, you are a genius. I didn't have the presence of mind to realize Klaus, our Nazi comrade, could help us escape from this Millsaap Flour Mill and this town of Marston. But, you realized how the nerd could be our 'patsy'. Please forgive me for all the snide and derogatory remarks I have made about you during the past several months."

Gerhard paused, then admitted, "I've been beside myself with worry and anguish about our dilemma here at this mill. But if your plan works we will soon be back in our birthplace. But what is our next move? Are you sure Klaus will contact us or will he leave us stranded here knee deep in wheat flour?"

"Remember, Gerhard, he always had a standing rule to communicate with us by flashing a message from the tower once every month on the 15th."

"Yah, last month he flashed the word 'Soon'."

"Recently his messages have expressed his fear of being exposed and arrested by the Americans. I think the time is near when he will just disappear and not appear at the laboratory."

"Also, he operates under an assumed name and has an important job at the Marston Optical Company, Gerhard. He knows the senior managers and laboratory workers at the company. I'm thinking Klaus will suggest and provide a way for the three of us to just disappear from here some dark night and eventually end up back home."

"What is Klaus's undercover name, the name he uses at the optical company?"

"It's hard to pronounce but it rhymes with the word simple, and has 'Mc' in front, perhaps McPimple; no, it's more like McDimple.... No, I remember now. His acquired name is Nevin McWhimple."

"What a stupid name.But it is rather appropriate. If he can help us disappear we will call him Nevin McAble. Horst, you may have exposed your genius and experienced another explosion of creative brain cells."

"What are you talking about?"

"Never mind; how will Nevin McWhimple, I mean McAble, help us now?"

"Lean over close to me, Gerhard. As you just said, my ingenious mind has given birth to another great idea. Come closer, we must be discreet and private in our conversations. The other four workers have just arrived for the morning shift. Now listen up—here is my plan."

# Chapter 3

O N THE NEXT WEDNESDAY AFTERNOON, under a blanket of dark, fast-moving cumulus clouds, the Marston County jail edifice appeared dark, dreary and foreboding to the few pedestrians passing by on their way to shops and businesses on the town square. Built of brick and Indiana limestone, the three-tiered building housing the jail cells and sheriff's offices stood as a secure sentinel reminding residents of the constant presence of protective law enforcement.

Just beyond the massive wood, steel-reinforced front door of the jail and forward a few steps in a dimly-lighted hallway, then to the left, Sheriff Byron Neverfine stirred on his massive upholstered chair. Glancing at the large, brass-encased, three-legged clock sitting on his desk he jumped up, gathered a few papers and scurried next door to the conference room.

The usual group of men making up his 'cabinet' had already arrived. He heard the members loudly discussing the recent apprehension and capture of Red Fox and his two underlings, Bruno and Udo.

"Good afternoon to you all," he announced loudly as he entered the room and approached the side table supporting the coffee maker. Fresh doughnuts purchased by Inspector Snooper that morning at the Never Drip Coffee Shop tempted everyone as they walked by the table.

"Hello, Sheriff. Speaking for everyone I can say it is good to be back here in our strategy room where we consumed many hours plotting the capture of Red Fox," said Captain Firmly with enthusiasm.

"Yes, I agree, and thank you, Captain Firmly, for your assistance with his apprehension and that vote of confidence."

"Sheriff, will Sam and Howie join us this afternoon?" asked Spade Digger. "I haven't seen either of the two detectives for days."

At that moment before the sheriff could respond the detectives shuffled through the door and quietly sat down at the side of the table next to the sheriff's chair.

"Good afternoon to all cabinet members and to both of you, Howie and Sam," the sheriff offered in a monotone. "Thanks for attending this meeting of the sheriff's cabinet. Howie, if you would, please jot down a written summary of our discussion and decisions as we proceed this afternoon. You can use the backs of the sheets from last year's 1947 calendar."

His coffee mug filled to the brim, the sheriff, walking briskly plopped down in his large chair located at the end of the large oval-shaped table constructed of solid oak. Rapping his coffee mug on the table top he informed, "Today, gentlemen we need to discuss some new information I have received recently concerning the property located at 404 Appalling Street. I believe this revelation is important and we need to decide if we should ignore the news or perhaps decide if the information merits our immediate attention."

Suddenly the room quieted, each member's attention focused on the sheriff.

"Start at the beginning, Sheriff," suggested Inspector Snooper, ignoring the sheriff's introductory remarks. "Share with this group of men our recent conversation at The Never Drip Coffee Shop."

"Yes, thank you, Snooper, that is my intention."

Glancing around the table and making eye contact with each member, the sheriff related, "A few days ago Mrs. Gertrude Everlite, the neighbor on the east side of the Ovid Prudely Mansion, appeared at my office. She seemed distressed, distraught and anxious to talk."

"What seemed to be bothering her?" asked Spade. "As far as we know everyone involved with Red Fox is either dead, in jail, in process of being deported or living in New Mexico under police supervision."

"It seems that during the last several days Mrs. Everlite has remembered some disturbing events that happened months ago at the Prudely Mansion.....Now picture in your minds this scene....Being a light sleeper she recalls waking and seeing lights flashing on and off usually at midnight or shortly thereafter." The sheriff lifted his coffee mug and slowly sipped the steaming brew.

He added, "These intermittent and sporadic flashings of light seemed to emanate from the top of the tower built into the northeast corner of the Prudely home."

The cabinet members shuffled their positions on the well-worn, straight-backed, cane-bottomed chairs. Placing their coffee mugs on the table top in unison they turned to face the sheriff more directly.

Continuing, the sheriff reminded, "As you all will remember from your many hours on the Prudely property, this tower is the silo-type structure that rises from the ground to a point above the roof line of the mansion. The roof of the tower is conical in shape and at the apex a weather vane is attached, featuring a running squirrel. At least six rather narrow glass windows, measuring approximately 12 inches wide and 24 inches tall, formed to match the curved shape of the tower walls are built into the structure."

"That's correct," remarked Howie. "The slate roof is conical and rises to a center point that supports the squirrel running in the direction of the prevailing wind. Sheriff, your description agrees with the photographs of the mansion. The photos plainly show the narrow, curved windows near the top of the structure."

"I, too, have admired that tower with those windows at the top," noted Captain Firmly. "That style of architecture gives the mansion prestige and a sense of protection and security. The rugged appearance is a reminder of 'in-vogue' Victorian design and construction in use during the years from 1890 to 1910."

"Before we continue this conversation," suggested the sheriff, "let's consider the following information related to the recent happenings at the mansion located at 404 Appalling Street, especially the people who have inhabited the structure during the past several years. Howie, please distribute a copy of this document to each member of the cabinet."

The sheriff then added, "This list, compiled by Inspector Snooper, Detectives Sam and Howie and myself summarizes the succinct outcomes of our recent investigation of the Prudely property and the activities of Red Fox and his associates therein during the past few years:

-First, the mansion and carriage house, built in 1900 using the English tradition as a model, have been viewed for years as a landmark and focal point by the citizens of Marston.

-Second, the home, remodeled during the 1930's by owners Ovid and Samantha Prudely, served as an employment office for several years during the 1930's and early 1940's.

-Third, several innovative changes and alterations built into the structure prompted our scrutiny of the home's interior. During our investigation members of this cabinet formed the opinion that the Prudely's may have utilized certain features of the altered rooms to kidnap selected applicants seeking employment. We believe some of these job-seekers ended up in situations not of their choosing. Lack of evidence ended our inquiry.

-Fourth, the German officer, Panzer Tank commander and undercover agent Colonel Helmut Schmidt, code name Red Fox, secretly and discretely occupied the premises and utilized an underground chemical laboratory beneath the carriage house for unusual chemical experiments.

-Fifth, products generated in this clandestine laboratory may have been used as skin-coloring agents. Also, Red Fox formulated a compound labeled BrainX, an insidious chemical concoction he hoped to use as a mind altering agent.

-Sixth, Red Fox died as a result of a fall in his jail cell.

-Seventh, Bruno, an underling of Red Fox, has been deported back to Germany.

-Eighth, Udo, a second patsy of Red Fox, returned to New Mexico. He earned his preaching license and now serves as visiting pastor sharing Jesus the Christ with inmates in jails in that state. His application for U.S. citizenship status is uncertain at this time."

As Sheriff Neverfine hesitated and reached for his coffee mug, Spade interrupted. "Yes, those comments constitute a good summary of what has absorbed our attention and labors for the past several weeks. We already know a lot about the property at 404 Appalling Street, Sheriff. Now, please tell us the main reason for this meeting today."

Slurping loudly as he drained his coffee mug the sheriff gave a condescending stare at Spade over the rim of the coffee mug. Then he glanced around the table at the expectant faces of the cabinet members. Setting the mug down on the oak surface with a bang he pulled several sheets of paper from a well-worn folder.

With an authoritative voice he began: "Here is the latest information that needs our attention regarding the property at the corner of Appalling and Mulberry Streets....Folks living in the proximity of the Prudely mansion are upset and have lodged a formal complaint with the Marston City Council."

Moving to page two he read, "Their complaint states and describes the deterioration of the abandoned Prudely mansion and carriage house. This decay is causing a perceived decrease in the value of nearby neighborhood properties.

The complaint also states and ends with this comment; 'The empty structures at 404 Appalling Street constitute an available and potential dangerous refuge for vagrants and curious teenagers who gain entrance to the buildings and remain for days at a time, smoke tobacco products and possibly 'shoot-up' drugs'."

Continuing, the sheriff stated, "Two weeks ago I received a copy of the notice the City Council published in the local newspaper. It states: 'Any person or entity claiming ownership interest in the property located at 404 Appalling Street should contact the Council within the next four weeks, or before November 15, 1948. Shortly thereafter, if no claims are forwarded, the mansion and carriage house will be demolished and the debris removed to the county landfill'."

"Do you think this sheriff's office or this cabinet needs to take any action in response to this notice?" asked Captain Firmly.

"Yes; Howie and Sam, I am ordering you two detectives to complete another thorough inspection of the two buildings destined for destruction at the 404 Appalling Street address."

"But, Sheriff," protested Sam, "Howie and I examined every room on all three levels of that mansion and also the carriage house. We have probed the walls, examined the floors and ceilings, closets and other storage areas. Our findings are part of the recent minutes of this Sheriff's Cabinet. What possible discoveries would warrant another search of the structures?"

"I know you and Howie must be weary of looking at the inside of those aging buildings. You both are probably thinking that a return scrutiny is a gross waste of time. However, to my knowledge you two detectives have not examined the round, silo-type tower built into the northeast corner of the house. That part of the house extends from the ground to a point above the roof line of the mansion."

"Also, Mrs. Everlite witnessed flickers of light emanating from the windows at the top of that structure," reminded Captain Firmly.

"Thank you, Captain. Now, Sam and Howie, make your investigation soon, perhaps tomorrow. Report your findings and observations at our cabinet meeting here in this room next Wednesday at one o'clock. You two detectives need to complete this responsibility quickly before the buildings are demolished....Oh, by the way, take Inspector Snooper with you as a representative of this Sheriff's Department. He is astute, professional and very cautious. He will keep you both focused on your objective."

Snooper, suddenly awake and attentive, stirred on his chair and blustered, "Sheriff, there have been several robberies reported by residents living in the Matter Park vicinity. Don't you think my professional time could be utilized more effectively by cruising that area and investigating these reported break-ins?"

"Yes, Snooper, by all means. After you assist Sam and Howie on their visit to the Prudely property at 404 Appalling Street, proceed to the area of reported robberies and make a thorough investigation. Report to this group next week on Wednesday....this meeting is adjourned."

Arising from his chair, Snooper, with a defeatist demeanor moped out of the conference room, his head down and his lips firm. Sam glanced at Howie, smiled and suggested, "Come on, partner, we need to formulate a plan for our re-visit to the Prudely property." Then he stepped firmly to Snooper's side and quietly suggested, "Inspector, be sure to pack your Smith and Wesson 38 Police Special for our venture tomorrow."

The inspector hurried out of the conference room door into the hallway. Sam and Howie followed at a rapid pace and glimpsed to their right. Snooper, at a fast gait, barged out of the jail through the massive, wood front door. They could hear him muttering to himself as the door slammed shut, "I need to settle my nerves. Perhaps a strong cup of java at The Never Drip Coffee Shop will lessen the anxiety building up in my psyche."

# Chapter 4

T HE NEXT MORNING DETECTIVES SAM and Howie met at their office located on Third Street directly across from the County Jail. As Howie inserted his office key into the door they glanced to their right. The County Courthouse, legal center for the county, stood as a commanding sentinel, dominating the entire central area of the town. A gentle breeze wafted through the numerous maple trees surrounding the edifice jiggling the colorful autumn leaves.

Hesitating for a moment Sam mused, "What a beautiful, peaceful sight, inspired by God."

Agreeing, Howie commented, "The autumn leaves sure are displaying a panorama of color."

Looking at the County Jail across the street Sam murmured, "By comparison the county lock-up appears drab and uninviting....I wonder if the sheriff is in his office at this early hour?"

Howie thought for a minute then answered, "I'm sure he is sitting at his monstrous desk thinking about this activity he assigned us to complete today. Snooper is probably standing in front of the sheriff's desk pleading for a last minute reprieve from joining our exciting venture."

"You could be right, Howie. Snoop is no doubt fretting about the prospect of his imagined dangers we might encounter in the tower at the Prudely mansion."

"Snoop certainly lacked enthusiasm yesterday when the sheriff ordered him to accompany us today."

"Right, but the sheriff rightly recalls the inspector's success during recent years in locating and subduing wanted fugitives. He knows Snooper always seems to be at the right place at crucial times to make the timely arrests."

"I agree, Sam; however, Snoop expressed zero interest in returning to 404 Appalling Street and helping us investigate the tower built into the northeast corner of the mansion."

"I know, but that's the only part of the structure we haven't explored, Howie."

As they entered their office, Howie, glancing at the clock mounted on the wall noticed the time, 7 o' clock. He retrieved the key for the front door to the Prudely Mansion from their wall safe secreted behind the picture of Jesus the Christ.

In a rather dejected mood he muttered, "Sam, why does the sheriff think we can uncover or discover additional information or items of importance at the Prudely mansion? We have already spent hours searching every nook and cranny in the mansion proper and the carriage house."

"I know," sighed Sam. "Every closet and piece of furniture has been searched and our observations and the contents noted. Evidently the sheriff believes the information recently related to him by Mrs. Everlite is important and warrants another search, concentrating our efforts this time inside the tower."

"Yeah, especially since we never sensed any reason to go inside the tower."

"I'm glad Inspector Snooper is going with us today; perhaps he can discover some new evidence of importance," suggested Sam.

Howie glanced out the front window toward the jail. He noted, "Here he comes now walking slowly from the jail. Uhh, Ohh, he almost stepped in front of the mayor's fast-moving, black limousine as he crossed 3rd Street. I don't think Snoop will be of much assistance to us today. He's frowning and his fists are clenched....perhaps his appeal to the sheriff for relief from today's assignment did not go well."

At that moment the Inspector entered the detectives' office. Without a word he plopped down in Sam's chair and stared at the portrait of Jesus hanging on the wall. "If you don't mind I'll just sit here for a few minutes and pray for our safety today."

"Good morning, Snoop," smiled Sam. "We are glad you are able to join us today." Stepping over and grasping Snoop's hands, he looked the inspector directly in his eyes and assured, "We appreciate your help today. Your two hands will be needed as we sort through whatever junk we find inside the tower."

Howie added, "Today we'll take the hammer, pry-bar and chopping axe from our truck into the house. Sam, we need to be prepared for any obstacle or barrier as we clear possible debris from our path. We'll chop that entry door of the tower into small pieces if necessary."

Snooper rose from his chair, sighed and said with a serious voice, "Sam, what items of value or interest can we possibly discover in that tower? The mansion has been vacant for years."

Continuing he lamented, "I'm not expecting to discover one bit of evidence that will intrigue us or further inform the members of the sheriff's cabinet."

"I agree, Inspector....we'll stumble over a jumble of cast-offs, broken furniture, worthless picture albums, old broken picture frames, empty bottles...basically junk to be carted to the landfill."

"Sam, I'll bet we can complete this mission in 30 minutes," added Howie. "Then we can enjoy a doughnut and coffee at the Never Drip Coffee Shop. Let's get going, Snooper."

The Inspector licked his lips and exited the office two steps ahead of Sam and Howie.

## Chapter 5

Parking their red pick-up truck at the accustomed space on Mulberry Street in front of the Prudely house, Sam turned off the ignition. The truck's powerful racing engine coughed twice, backfired once, shuddered, then settled into a wheezing state of assured quietness. Sliding off the well-worn leather seat the detectives and Inspector Snooper stood on the cracked concrete sidewalk in front of the gate structure made of twisted iron bars now rusted to an antiqued shade of muted red and grey.

"I can see why the neighbors are complaining about the condition of this property," offered Howie, gesturing toward the house and surrounding lawn area. "The once beautiful mansion and carriage house have deteriorated to the point of disgrace..... Sam, the wood shutters on the upstairs windows are hanging askew."

The trio stepped over broken tree limbs and weathered newspapers as they made their way toward the front door.

"Look, two windows on the east side of the house are broken.... Howie, use the Prudely house key. Let's try to open the front door."

After several minutes of twisting, banging, kicking and shoving the thick entry door grudgingly squeaked open. Brushing the spider webs aside the detectives entered the structure and stood silently in the foyer. A few seconds later the inspector, wide-eyed, slowly shuffled in and joined his comrades in the quiet, eerie and rather foreboding space.

"I now understand why we never turned left to approach the tower area," suggested Howie. "The magnificent gathering room located straight ahead with the huge fireplace and life-sized family portrait is so attractive and appealing we just naturally moved forward in that direction."

"This building could become a historic gem again with the proper restoration," commented Snooper.

Looking to his left, Sam suggested, "Here is the hallway leading in the direction of the tower. Let's see if we can locate the access door."

After a few steps Howie, wiping the spider webs from his face, pointed and shouted, "There it is! Would you look at the front of that huge door! The surface of the wood is painted to resemble the front of some large animal...Yes, it's a male black bear standing up on his rear legs!"

"And his green eyes are staring right at us!" shouted Snooper, retreating a step and pointing at the face of the bear. "And, look at the oversized nose stuck on his face! It's at least four or five inches long!"

Sam, using his shirt sleeve, wiped some of the accumulated dust and grime from the surface of the bear's painted face. Then the threesome stood transfixed, admiring the realistic image formed by an unknown artist.

Howie, still mesmerized by the bear's likeness, stood back and said, "Look, Snooper, the bear is facing us with his mouth wide open and his long teeth ready to bite anyone who dares to open this door."

"I'll bet the artist who painted the portrait over the fireplace in the gathering room also painted this impression of a bear," suggested Snooper, fascinated by the bear's image. "The rendition is very realistic and frightening."

"But where is the door knob?" asked Sam. "I don't see any way to open this door."

"You have the axe, Howie; start chopping," directed Snooper anxious to complete their assignment and vacate the mansion.

"Wait a minute," directed Sam. "That bear's nose is much larger than normal and protrudes forward. Why is the nose so prominent?... and, no door knob....Howie, grab that huge nose and pull."

The detective reached up and grasped the wood nose with both hands. He pulled, twisted and pushed with force. Suddenly, the nose broke free. Howie, still grasping the nose lurched backward, pulling several feet of rusted cable out from behind the thick wood.

The men could hear a loud click. Howie stood back a few feet and lunged forward, his shoulder colliding against the sturdy wood door. The bear-faced door broke free from its years of inactivity and opened wide with a loud squeaking, groaning sound. The detectives and Snooper stood with mouths open as if in a trance gawking at the scene in front of them.

# Chapter 6

ATTACHED TO THE OPPOSITE END of the cable a square metal bar had pivoted upward from a holding slot in the door jamb allowing the barrier with its painted bear face to swing open. The detectives deftly and slowly soft-shoed past the bear's image and entered the foreboding, shadowy space beyond.

Howie frowned as he inquisitively reached up and touched the bear's face, now minus a nose. Adequate light filtered into the area from the windows at the top of the tower allowing the visitors to view the interior of the tower. Looking beyond they could see littered on the wood floor a jumbled array of broken boards, empty gallon paint containers, dust-covered boxes, discarded parts of furniture, picture frames, dried-up flower arrangements and an upturned, rusted laundry tub.

"What a mess," declared Sam. "I don't think anyone has been in this area for months."

At one side several dusty sacks filled with unknown contents had been piled in a jumbled fashion covering a large space on the floor.

Howie, curious, suggested, "We can deal with the junk items later. Let's move those sacks over to one side." He stepped over to the collection of sacks that littered the floor, picked up one of the dust-covered items on top and brushed the accumulated dust off the front.

"Sam!" he yelled, "look at this bag! You can see the words, MILLSAAP FLOUR MILL, printed across the front! And, there just below," he pointed, "is a facsimile of the mill's exterior."

"That's strange, Howie, ...bags full of flour stored here in this long-vacant tower of the mansion at 404 Appalling Street. This location is a long distance from the milling operation on the Mississinewa River."

"What possible connection could have existed between this residence and The Millsaap Flour Mill?" continued Sam, wondering out loud.

"I don't know but Sheriff Neverfine will be interested in our findings...old sacks filled with flour dumped on the floor here in the tower of the Prudely mansion."

"Here is another larger bag, Sam!" yelled Howie as he separated one sack from the pile and brushed off the dust. "This bag holds 50 pounds of flour and it's so full the stitching at the seam has deteriorated and the bag split wide open."

"Go ahead and force the sack all the way open. Let's see why the seam on that bag split open."

"I'm not sure I should, Sam....Are we tampering with possible evidence?"

"I don't think so. The sheriff has authorized us to explore this tower. Break open the bag so we can see why it split wide open."

As Howie gradually separated the seam further the contents of the bag shifted and became visible. The detectives gasped in unison.

"Howie, there's a shrunken, dried-up body inside!" shouted Sam. "We are witnessing a shriveled-up corpse covered with flour!"

"Come back here, Snoop!" yelled Howie. "We haven't finished our investigation of this tower!"

The inspector, two steps outside the tower door and moving rapidly toward the exit, slowed, then reluctantly shuffled back to join the detectives.

"Snoop, you are as white as the flour inside that ruptured sack. Sit here on these full sacks and relax for a few moments."

"Don't touch any of the contents inside that open sack, Howie. If that object is indeed a dead person the sheriff will no doubt order a full inquiry."

"Should we stop our survey and report our findings to the sheriff or go ahead and examine the entire tower?" wondered Howie, gazing up at the peak of the tower.

"We need to complete our examination now," replied Sam. "See that metal, spiral staircase. That's how the Prudely's climbed to the top."

"Inspector," interrupted Howie with a firm voice, "since you are the representative of the sheriff's office, whatever can be seen from the top of this tower should be viewed first by you....so, up you go." Howie grabbed Snooper's arm and attempted to guide him to the base of the staircase.

"No way am I climbing up that rickety staircase. The small rusted steps offer no assurance of safety. It's evident from the accumulated dust that no one has mounted these stairs in years. The entire staircase could come crashing down with me tangled up in the middle of the mess." Snooper shrugged off Howie's hand and withdrew to be near the entrance door. Seeing the bear's face he grimaced and moved again to the far opposite side of the tower floor.

"All right," announced Sam, "I'll go up the first few steps. If the apparatus seems to be sturdy I'll continue climbing. Howie can follow and join me at the top."

Slowly, carefully, the two detectives mounted the rusted squeaky steps to the top of the tower. Howie, climbing a few steps behind commented, "Sam, the tower decreases in diameter as we approach the top."

"Yes, I would estimate the width here at the top to be about eight feet."

After climbing up the last few steps they stood on two-inch-thick boards covered with dust that comprised a circular wooden platform, a sort of walkway. Suddenly, Howie stopped, pointed and yelled, "Sam, what is that?"

Their eyes and mouths popped open as they observed a human-like form sitting on a stool. Bending forward with the right eye up against the eyepiece of a telescope the figure seemed to be aiming the instrument outward through one of the rectangular panes of glass.

"Sam, are we dreaming? Is that figure a mannequin sitting on a stool with it's right eye up against the eyepiece of a telescope?"

"Perhaps, but why would a stuffed form resembling a human body be seated up here looking through a telescope...and, dressed in such outlandish clothes?"

"I certainly can't answer that question. Let's see if we can determine the distant object being observed by the mannequin."

Howie reached forward and with his handkerchief began to wipe off the film-like coating that had accumulated on the inside surface of the curved panels of glass built into the wall of the tower.

As they squinted and gazed out through the glass panels, Sam yelled, "I can't believe what we are seeing. Here in a circular space at the top of this tower constructed at the corner of the Prudely mansion, we can see the tops of houses for quite a distance.....Oh, hi, Snooper. I'm glad you decided to join us."

"Well, I felt rather uneasy sitting down there on the floor next to that corpse in the flour bag. So, I decided to join you two detectives up here."

Turning his attention back to the telescope, Howie suggested, "You are right, Sam. Let's focus on the entire scene before us. We need to remember as much detail as possible so we can document our findings for our report to members of the sheriff's cabinet. ....How far, with the advantage of the telescope, could the mannequin or perhaps a real person, see in the distance?"

"The form seated on the stool seems to be looking in a northeast direction. At one time, Howie, with the curved windows cleared of dust and film, the person looking through this telescope could probably see over the rooftops of neighbor's homes, and possibly view the northeast area of Marston, the Matter Park and a portion of the Mississinewa River."

Inspector Snooper became curious and moved closer to the figure sitting on the metal stool. He suddenly became erect, took a deep breath and blurted out, his words coming in stuttered, shouted syllables; "As I look closer the seated form looks less like a mannequin and more like a petite human form! The frayed clothing strips are mismatched and hang on the form as tattered shreds! The miss-matched top and pants seem to be hanging in ragged ribbons printed in stick figures of various colors! Sam and Howie, that figure is a dead person-- a human

'TATTERBITTY'!"

"A what!" yelled Sam.

"A TatterBitty! A human form dressed in tattered strips of cloth and bits of old, printed colorful rags!"

Ignoring the inspector's spirited revelation, Howie yelled, "Come on, Sam; let's get out of here. We need to climb down the staircase and write up our report that we will give to the members of the sheriff's cabinet."

"Wait a minute, Howie, I just noticed that box over there on the walkway, the metal container next to the metal tripod supporting the telescope....Do you suppose there is anything of interest inside?"

"We'll soon find out. Hand me the screwdriver you have in your back pocket."

After several minutes of prying and jabbing the lid popped off, revealing a boxy instrument of some sort. Sam gently lifted the object out of the box and turned it over so they could see all sides.

Finally, Howie blurted out, "Sam, in your hands you are holding some sort of device with a lens and light bulb inside. Hand the box to me for a minute."

After Howie had investigated the object, he offered, "I think this apparatus is some type of lamp used as a signaling device. Sam, is it possible Mrs. Everlite saw flashes of light blinking from this instrument, perhaps generated by the instrument and triggered by the TatterBitty to send signals to some distant objective?"

"Hmmm....You may be right, Howie. We'll report this discovery to the sheriff's cabinet and let the members decide how to proceed.... Leave the box and the contents right where we found it. Come on, we'll climb back down to the main floor and prepare our written report."

Sam and Howie sat on sacks of flour with the Millsaap logo as they jotted down observations pertaining to their visit to the mansion tower. A few minutes later Sam looked around, then asked, "Where is Inspector Snooper?"

The detectives discovered the inspector had vanished. Stepping out through the tower door now open wide, they viewed the inspector rushing toward the entry door to the mansion. As Snooper rushed out of the building he resembled a running track star, his eyes fixed on the sanctity of the red pick-up truck.

# Chapter 7

❧

O N THAT NEXT WEDNESDAY, OCTOBER 20th, 1948, members of Sheriff Neverfine's cabinet settled in on their usual squeaky, cane bottom chairs around the large oval conference table. The aroma of freshly brewed coffee drifted lazily among the members engaged in loud conversation. Their laughter could be heard in the sheriff's office a short distance away down a dimly-lit hallway. He sighed. The time had arrived for him to step to the conference room and join his colleagues.

Clomping heavily on the oak flooring he entered the room and approached the side table supporting the coffee urn, a tray of doughnuts and utensils. His boisterous entrance could not be ignored. The cabinet members shifted their chairs and sat expectantly their attention fixed upon the sheriff's commanding physique.

Anxious to hear the summary of the inspection report detectives Sam, Howie and Inspector Snooper had completed at the Prudely mansion the group quieted immediately. Every member had mixed expectations. Could the examination of the tower structure possibly yield any information of value? Everyone around the table had quietly pre-judged the results of the inspection efforts- 'today's report and conversation would be boring and of no further consequence to them as lawmen'. They assumed a relaxed posture and continued talking with a soft jovial attitude.

"Good afternoon, Sheriff," greeted Spade. "I see you have only one doughnut on your plate. Are you on a diet?"

"Errr, yes in a way...I need to lose a few pounds," responded the sheriff, squinting and glaring with disgust over the top of his glasses at the mortician. "Now, let's get to work. The main item on our agenda today is to hear the report from Sam, Howie and Inspector Snooper. As you all no doubt remember I ordered them to re-visit the Prudely mansion and inspect the interior of the tower, that round structure on the northeast corner of the house.....Alright, detectives, you're on.What are the impressions resulting from your inspection?"

The cabinet members exhaled, leaned back and reached for their half-filled coffee mugs not expecting much new information. Inspector Snooper tried to shrink down into his chair to become as unnoticed and innocuous as possible.

Howie glanced at their hastily-prepared report and began: "Last Thursday, October 7th, Detective Sam and I followed up on the directive from this group, that is, to inspect the tower structure built into the northeast corner of the Prudely mansion, located at 404 Appalling Street, here in Marston. Inspector Snooper accompanied us as a representative of this sheriff's department."

"Yes, yes, Howie, enough review of the property in question. Proceed to your observations and findings," ordered the sheriff as he loudly drained his coffee mug.

47

"Entering the Prudely house we walked to our left and faced the entrance door opening to the tower proper. Since we possessed no entry key we encountered a real problem.....how do we access the tower?"

"Yeah," chimed in Sam. "Picture this....some artist had painted a portrait of the frontal view of a huge bear standing erect on the surface of the door including the huge head! From the eyes a piercing gaze stared straight at us. Also, the substantial wood door lacks a lever, knob, keyhole or any common means to gain entry to the tower."

"So, since you couldn't open the door your mission ended at that point," suggested Captain Firmly, draining his coffee mug.

"No, no! Howie and I examined the front surface of the door with our hands. We noticed the bear's nose seemed to be quite oversized, perhaps too large in proportion to the bear's head."

"So, don't most bears have huge noses?" asked Spade, with a slight smirk.

Howie asked, "Have you ever examined a bear's nose, Spade?"

The conference room became very quiet. Spade became stoic. Howie continued, "Sam and I, in turn, grabbed the wooden nose, turned and twisted and pulled on it but with no success- the door remained shut."

Still speaking dramatically Howie emphasised, "Finally, I grabbed the huge nose with both hands, placed my shoes on the front surface of the door and jerked....the nose broke free and I fell backward holding the bear's nose in my hands....Sam, tell our comrades about the attachment fastened to the rear end of the cable."

"A metal cable attached to the nose extended through the door. The opposite end activated a lever. When we pulled on the cable the lever swung upward out of a slot and the door could be opened. We gasped as we viewed the murky interior of the tower. Our eyes gradually adjusted to the darkened area. As we stepped inside we discovered many objects of various sizes and shapes."

The cabinet members suddenly sat upright, caught up with the detectives' revelations.

"Well, I'll be...." muttered Spade. "So, the only means of entry to the tower is to twist a bear's nose and pull on the attached cable. That action lifts a securing metal bar."

"That's right," smiled Sam, pleased the mortician correctly summarized the procedure to access the tower.

"Well, now that we are inside the tower, what do we find?" asked Captain Firmly with more interest and courtesy.

"When we cautiously stepped inside the rather dark tower we stepped over cardboard boxes and around old broken wood crates, empty bottles and scraps of paper," added Sam.

"Well," interjected the sheriff, "the Prudely's probably decided the tower had scant practical use so they used the space as a dumping area for items no longer needed."

"But," cautioned Sam, standing up and excitedly waving his arms, "although that usage happened to be our initial opinions, further investigation revealed some very suspicious and strange items to be found in any storage space at any residence."

Now the lawmen became wide awake and alert. "Sam, go ahead and describe your subsequent findings," demanded Captain Firmly.

Sam nodded to his partner. "Howie, tell our colleagues about the objects we stumbled over when we moved further into the tower."

"We found several cotton sacks filled with white wheat flour. The sacks, strewn about the floor just inside the entryway covered about one-half of the floor space......Now, Inspector, describe the contents of one large cotton sack that had split open at the seam."

Snooper jolted upright, straightened his posture and blurted in a loud voice, "Gentlemen, are you prepared for the shock of your professional lives?" …..Standing and leaning on the table with both hands he gazed at the face of each cabinet member now sitting with increased expectancy. Hesitating for a few more seconds to create anxiety he then waved his arms about and shouted, "We found a long-dead corpse stuffed into a fifty pound flour sack and dumped there on the tower floor!"

The conference room became very quiet for what seemed to be several long minutes. Then suddenly the room became alive with loud talking, questions and expressions of amazement.

Finally, Sheriff Neverfine pounded on the table top with his empty coffee mug to restore quiet and ordered, "Alright! alright! Detectives, you found a few old cotton sacks full of flour, and one that seems to contain a decomposed body. No doubt you discovered the remains of a dead opossum or a large dog placed in the sack as a means of disposal. Did you at this point terminate your investigation?"

"No!" answered Sam, in a loud voice and still standing. "That discovery occurred on the floor of the tower. Howie, describe our amazement as we climbed the spiral staircase and reached the top of the structure."

When Howie hesitated a few seconds to assemble his notes, the sheriff, looked at his watch and demanded, "Well, Howie, go ahead, start talking....I can't imagine you found anything at the top of that unused tower that is important to our discussion today."

"Quite to the contrary, Sheriff. When we finally reached the top and stepped on the wood planks that serve as a circular walkway we stopped and stared, shocked at what we viewed."

"Yeah," added Sam, "sitting on a metal stool, a rather small figure clad in tattered bits and strips of colorful clothing seemed to be looking through a telescope directed toward the northeast region of Marston, perhaps the Matter Park area and a small portion of the Mississinewa River."

"Wait a minute, Sam," cautioned Captain Firmly, "are you suggesting this object looking through the telescope is a corpse, not a stuffed image?"

"Right....at first we assumed the object sitting on the stool to be a mannequin. But, after a further up-close inspection we presumed the figure to be another corpse. Since the form is clad with frayed and tattered strips and bits of colorful clothing, Inspector Snooper labeled the person, 'The TatterBitty'."

"A what!" yelled Spade, derisively.

The inspector bristled, straightened his posture and forcefully replied, "The label, TatterBitty, aptly describes the figure sitting on the stool. Long strands of frayed multi-colored ribbons of cotton material constitute the clothing for the figure. You can find the words tatter and bitty in the dictionary. The definitions of these two words aptly describe the clothing we observed on the subject sitting there looking through a telescope."

After a long pause the cabinet members finally shifted their positions on the cane-bottom chairs. They looked at each other seeking some common direction. Finally after a rather extended, awkward, embarrassing silence, Captain Firmly leaned forward, pointed his finger at Sam and asked, "In your opinion, considering the appearance of the object sitting on the stool, are we dealing with a clad dummy or a human corpse?"

"Howie and I have discussed at length our impressions of The TatterBitty. At this point we believe there are two corpses in the tower....one in the split-open flour sack and the second is sitting on a stool at the top of the tower looking through a telescope."

"Your findings, if authentic, create a major new facet of our investigation into the activities of former inhabitants of the Prudely mansion," remarked the sheriff. "Spade, as soon as possible, remove the two purported corpses from the Prudely tower and place them in refrigeration at your mortuary.....Also, using my authority contact the local medical examiner and ask that person for professional assistance. Consult medical and mortuary professionals in nearby cities, especially Indianapolis, to help you as needed in your examination and identification of the corpses. Return to this group next Wednesday and report your findings."

"Also, Captain Firmly, please assist Mr. Digger when he enters the tower to retrieve the bodies," directed the sheriff. "Ask your specialists at Indiana State Police headquarters to help you with this case. Take whatever photographs that will be helpful to reach conclusions regarding this investigation."

"Yes, I will follow through with your requests, Sheriff. I am intrigued with the description of the person looking through the telescope, the so-called TatterBitty. Also, we will try to map out the area under the scope's field of observation."

"Sam and Howie," continued the sheriff, "research and examine all the sacks of flour you discovered on the floor inside the tower. Try to determine why they happened to be at that location. Also, assist Mr. Digger if he requests your help by pulling on the bear's nose to enter the tower so he can remove The TatterBitty."

Continuing, his eyes fixed on the detectives, he added, "It seems impossible to stuff a person's body inside a flour sack. Visit the Millsaap Flour Mill. Take the Inspector and Frank Overbaring with you. Snooper's presence will give you the official backing of this office."

"Also, detectives, perhaps Frank can take a few photographs giving us further evidence of the workings at the flour mill. Be nosy. Question the owner and workers. Try to find out why flour sacks, one with the Millsaap Flour Mill's depiction on it ended up in the tower of the Prudely mansion with a possible human body inside."

"What about the flashing lights that Mrs. Everlite observed coming from the tower?" asked Snooper.

"Yes, thank you, Inspector; that will be your responsibility. Report back to this group next Wednesday, October 27th....Ask Sam and Howie to assist you, if necessary."

Glancing around the table the sheriff concluded, "Thank you all for your professional efforts as we attempt to solve this case of The TatterBitty, and the corpse discovered inside the Millsaap Flour Mill sack found on the floor of the Prudely tower."

He stopped and looked over the top of his glasses in the direction of Snooper's chair as he added, "Now, Inspector Sneupenhauger, do you have any further comments to wrap up our session today?"

The inspector's chair, however, appeared quite empty. He had already vacated the conference room. His exit and fast trip to the bathroom located in the rear of the jail would be his most rapid ever.

# Chapter 8

ON THAT BRIGHT FRIDAY MORNING, October 22nd, Sam's red pick-up truck loaded with an odd assortment of personnel, bumped easily in a northerly direction along Washington Street toward the Matter Park area. The Millsaap Flour Mill, located across from the park on the east bank of the Mississinewa River would be their first and most important stop. Ample sunshine had pushed the temperature up to 80 degrees making the ride tolerable for the two men riding and bouncing about in the truck's bed.

Howie, seated on the passenger side, turned, faced Sam and suggested, "I'm glad Inspector Snooper followed through on the sheriff's directions and agreed to accompany us on this inspection trip to the flour mill."

Sam, staring straight ahead and pressing his right foot down firmly on the gas pedal replied, "I think the Inspector feels more comfortable about his assignment since we are accompanying him. The Inspector represents the sheriff's office giving us the authority for the visit. As detectives we can do the snooping and ask the difficult questions. Hopefully the Inspector will be our leader and act as our moderator."

"That gesture is appropriate since he called the Millsaap Mill owner, Mr. Silas Canbee, and made these arrangements for us to visit the mill and ask questions about the operation."

"I'm also glad Frank Overbaring, the photographer for the *Marston Tribune*, agreed to go along with us today. He will, no doubt, write an interesting and informative article for the newspaper with supporting photos."

"Well, here we are at the Mill. I'll park on the south side of the building next to the river."

Jumping out of the truck the foursome stood as a group gazing at the weathered wooden structure. "The mill sure seems a lot larger and taller when viewed up close," suggested Frank, slipping the camera's strap over his shoulder. Pointing he added, "There are three main tiers plus a cupola with windows on the fourth floor."

"Well, Snooper, we can't learn much standing here. Go ahead and lead us inside to meet Mr. Canbee," suggested Howie.

Marching in single file the group stepped across the crushed limestone- covered parking lot. Snooper, in the forefront and stepping forcefully, looked at his pocket watch. He increased his gait as he led the small group toward the only visible small entryway. As they approached the door they noticed it seemed to be made of slabs of tree bark covered with rusted sheet metal. Above that entrance a single, crudely-painted word,'Office', indicated they had moved in the right direction.

The plain-appearing building, lacking paint and abutting the rushing waters of the Mississinewa River, provided an appropriate backdrop for the huge water wheel. As the diverted river water moved rapidly along the wood trough, called a raceway or sluice, and splashed against wood paddles the water wheel rotated turning a complex arrangement of gears, wood drums and axles. As it turned an unusual combination of sounds erupted ranging from thuds, squeaks, bumps and water splashes in the midst of hearty voices shouted by busy workers.

Pushing the door open with assumed authority, Snooper marched forward and extended his hand to the sole occupant of the small entry room. He blurted out, "Good morning, Mr. Canbee. My name is Inspector Hershel Sneupenhauger serving with Sheriff Neverfine at the Gurant County Jail. We have an appointment to visit with you in fifteen minutes at 10 o'clock."

"I'm sorry, Hershel, I'm Quincy. That's my truck parked by the unloading dock. It's loaded with sacks of wheat from my farm near the town of Van Buren. The wheat will be ground into flour. Mr. Canbee, the manager of the mill, holds forth yonder, thru that entryway. But be aware, the rickety door came off the hinges a few days ago and fell on Mr. Canbee's head causing an eruption of unkindly words."

Thanking Quincy for his timely caution, Snooper edged the green door open a few inches. Seeing a dour-faced, dumpy, oval-shaped man clad in green bib overalls decorated with white vertical stripes he marched on inside and extended his right hand in greeting.

"Good morning, Mr. Canbee. Our delegation from the sheriff's office is here as scheduled. My name is Hershel Sneupenhauger; my friends call me Snooper. I want you to meet Sam Hames and Howie Newbald, detectives associated with the sheriff's office.

Also, standing behind Sam is Mr. Frank Overbaring, distinguished photographer for the *Marston Tribune*."

Giving a slight bow, the overall-clad mill manager changed his facial expression and extended his hand in turn to all four visitors and warmly said, "Welcome to The Millsaap Flour Mill. At first I thought you all represented the group of citizens from the park protesting the drab appearance of this mill. I am most pleased to meet with all of you to explain and provide information regarding this landmark structure, its function and the history it represents..... Now, please follow me and I will provide background narrative that will help explain the operation of the mill before we tour the facility. Let's move to the workers' break-room where we can talk in a more quiet area."

Proceeding to a small, rustic enclosed area, Mr. Canbee pointed to three split-log benches, rough-hewn long ago from nearby oak trees, and suggested, "Please find a seat."

After a few minutes he gestured to his left and intoned, "This wall of glass enables visitors and workers to view the turning water wheel that powers this mill's mechanism."

After allowing about ten minutes for the group to view and absorb the movements of the axles, gears, wheels and grinding stone, Mr. Canbee reached into a cooling case and brought out five bottles of Jiffy Cola. He popped off the caps using the opener attached to the front of the cooler.

As he handed the beverages to the visitors he approached Frank and said, "Mr. Overbaring, please feel welcome to photograph any part of the mechanism and the process of milling. Your pictures and accompanying articles occurring in *The Marston Tribune* will complement our efforts here as we serve our public. We are proud of the Mill's history and its past and continuing contribution to the local culture and economy."

"Thank you, Mr. Canbee, for your hospitality. Can you briefly explain the past history of this mill?" asked Sam.

"Yes, and I will also attempt to show you the function of each major part of the mill as the business operates and serves the community."

"How old is the mill?" asked Frank.

"Old records in the local Gurant County Library suggest this mill may date back to the mid 1800's. Early sketches indicate this structure at one time served as a sawmill."

"Are the terms 'gristmill' and 'flour mill' appropriate for any mill that grinds grain?" asked Sam.

"Yes, that term can refer to any facility where farmers bring in their grain and are given back ground cornmeal or wheat flour minus a small amount, called 'the miller's toll' to pay for the milling services...now, let's move on out and view the moving machinery as the grain is processed."

Proceeding to the grinding area Mr. Canbee hesitated, then gestered as he explained, "Most mills in England and in this country have been and are currently water-powered."

He pointed to a trough-like structure leading to the large water wheel and stated, " When the sluice gate you see yonder is opened water from the Mississinewa River rushes forward and engages the paddles on the vertical water wheel causing it to rotate. A gear wheel is mounted on the same axle. This wheel drives the grinding millstone and a shaft that runs vertically from here to the top of the building powering a hoist among other features."

"How fast is the millstone turning?" asked Frank, aiming his camera.

"The top grinding stone is the 'runner' and turns about 120 revolutions per minute. The bottom stone, called the 'bed', is fixed."

"Let's assume I am a local farmer who has arrived with a truck loaded with sacks of wheat to be milled," suggested Howie. "What happens next?"

"The sacks filled with grain are removed from the farmer's truck and placed on the hoist that lifts the sacks to the top of the mill, powered by the gear wheel. The grain in the sacks is emptied into bins. When a slide at the bottom of a bin opens the wheat falls through a chute down into a hopper located directly above the 'runner' millstone. From the hopper the grain is directed to the surface between the runner and the fixed stone. The milled wheat flour is collected in sacks on the floor below."

"How many employees are required to keep this operation 'humming'?" asked Sam."

Four men operate and oversee the mill's operation during the daytime, receiving the grain, processing the wheat or corn and filling the sacks or bags with meal or flour. Two employees have the night shift. Their responsibility includes cleaning and maintaining the building and the grinding mechanism."

Howie glanced sideways at Sam, then added, "Do you package the milled grain in sacks of different sizes?"

"Yes," answered Mr. Canbee, holding up an empty sack, the front printed with the MILLSAAP logo and sketch of the mill. "This cotton sack holds 25 pounds of flour. Smaller filled sacks of flour are sold to variety and grocery stores."

"How much flour do the largest sacks contain?" pressed Howie.

"A few of our customers are restaurant or bakery owners. They buy our flour in 50 pound bags. I might add the larger empty sacks are popular with women who wash them and make dresses with the material. Children can be seen wearing colorful clothing made from our flour sacks."

"Can we proceed to the top floor and the cupola?" asked Sam, anxious to determine if he could see the Prudely mansion tower from this location.

"Sure, we can step on the hoist and the gear wheel will turn a wooden drum that winds up a rope to power the hoist and us to the top floor. Then we can proceed up a few steps to the cupola."

Five minutes later the group, gazing out through the glass windows, remained silent for several minutes absorbing the magnificent vista spread out before them.

"What a sight," remarked Sam. Turning to Howie, he pointed in a southwesterly direction and exclaimed. "Look, we can see over the house tops for a long distance....Yes, there in plain view is the tower of the Prudely house."

"Mr. Canbee, what is the purpose of this room?" asked Howie?

"I learned from the previous manager of this mill that this room has no practical function related to the milling of grain. As you have noticed the hoist only lifts to the third floor. We had to climb a series of steps to arrive here on the top floor."

Silas added..... "This room provides a place for customers to relax while waiting for the mill to process their wheat or rye into flour or corn into meal. Also, this cupola may have been added for architectural purposes to enhance the boxy appearance of the mill."

Inspector Snooper pointed to the rolled-up shades above the windows and added, "Your suggestion that the space may have been utilized as a waiting room has merit....all the windows can be shaded with those blinds making the room more comfortable on sunny days."

Sam grabbed a cord hanging from the center of one blind and pulled the shade down. Smiling he agreed, "Yes, the blind would assist in keeping the room cooler during hot periods."

Then he nudged Howie and whispered, "Notice the round and rectangular holes in the blind."

"Yeah, the holes may be age related."

Howie poked Sam and pointed to an oblong box resting on the floor in a distant corner. Then he asked Mr. Canbee, "Does that object lying over there on the floor have a purpose?"

"I have no idea," replied the mill manager with a blank look on his face. "I haven't been up here in this room for many months, perhaps years. Let's see if we can identify the object."

Pulling the box forward out of the corner Mr. Canbee dropped to his knees and began to unwrap the canvas cover. Then a few binding cords broke loose. A can of paint and a small paint brush tumbled out on the floor. Then Silas reached inside and held up what appeared to be a metal-encased instrument with a protruding tube and glass lens attached to the front end.

"What in the world is that?" gasped Snooper.

Frank Overbaring reached for his camera.

# Chapter 9

THE NEXT MORNING WHILE SITTING in their detective office and writing a summary of their visit to the flour mill, Howie looked at his partner and suggested, "Sam, today would be the best time to follow the Sheriff's directive and make a quick return visit to the Prudely mansion. We can examine closely the contents of those flour sacks piled on the floor of the tower."

"I agree, but we can't just dump the flour on the tower floor and leave the mess for someone else to clean up."

"Right, Sam; let's stop at the NeedMore Store and purchase two large garbage containers. We can inspect each bag then dump the flour in the garbage cans. The Marston disposal truck can haul away the contents to the city dumping area."

"Good idea; it's 10 a. m., let's get going and complete this messy job...we'll probably look like snowmen when we are finished with this job. As I recall the Sheriff did have a weak smile on his face when he assigned the task to us."

One hour later the detectives opened the front door of the mansion and marched left toward the tower. Howie grabbed the bear's nose, pulled lustily, disengaging the locking lever. Dragging the two large garbage containers into the base area of the tower they set to work. Howie opened his jack knife.

"Sam, I'll slit each of the cotton sacks open at the front and you can reach inside to examine the flour to determine if any foreign objects are hidden inside."

Several minutes later Sam, on his knees, had examined the flour inside ten cotton sacks. His hands and arms were coated with flour. "Howie, I don't think we will find anything but flour in these sacks."

"I hope you are right."

Then as he thrust his hand into sack number eleven Sam's eye brows bounced up as he felt a substance different from the powdery white material. He hesitated then grasped the object, pulled it out of the bag, straightened his posture and yelled, "Howie, I found something!....It looks like a small paper bag!"

"Is there anything inside the bag?" asked Howie.

"Yeah, it feels like a round, hard circular object. Wait a minute.... use your jack knife and cut this paper bag open. Then maybe we can identify the item."

A few minutes later, Howie held up a round piece of glass, slightly thicker at the center. "Sam, I think this piece of glass is a lens for a large camera."

"Possibly; let's examine the remainder bags of flour. Perhaps we'll find more objects hidden inside."

"Wait a minute, Sam. I just noticed the printing on the front of this cotton bag that contained the piece of glass. See, the printed facsimile of the **M**illsaap Mill has been altered slightly."

"What are you talking about, Howie? This cotton bag looks just like all the other sacks."

"No, Sam, look closely.... the **M** letter in the word **M**illsaap is different than the same letter on the other sacks. The right-hand leg of the **M** letters is darkened. Someone has taken a pen with black ink or a paint brush with black paint to make the printed sketch of the **M**ill different."

"I see what you mean....the letter in the **M**illsaap name now appears black on the right leg."

"You have made a very interesting and perhaps important observation, Howie. Set the piece of glass aside. We need to examine all the sacks. There may be more flour sacks with glass pieces hidden inside."

By noontime the detectives had slit open and examined the contents of each remaining sack. In the process they discovered three more cotton sacks with the letter **M** darkened, each containing a round glass specimen similar to the original discovery.

"Sam, I've placed all four circular glass objects in this empty flour bag, a sack with the altered logo on the front. We need to vacate this tower and take the bag to our office. We can write up our report for the sheriff's cabinet. Then we need to go home and hope a good shower will wash off this coating of flour."

Two hours later Sam received a phone call at his apartment. With concern Howie stated, "Sam, we now have four small paper bags in our possession, each containing a round glass disc. We don't know the function of the glass objects although they do resemble some type of lens."

"Yeah, I know...Why are you calling me at 12 o'clock? Do you want to meet me at the Never Drip Coffee Shop for lunch?"

"Maybe later, but right now I have a suggestion as to determining the purpose for the four glass pieces."

"Well, go ahead, what's on your mind?"

"I know a scientist who works at The Marston Optical Company, on Adams Street. His name is Nevin McWhimple. My wife and I see him every Sunday at The Methodist Church where preacher Rob Kneel holds forth. A follower of Jesus the Christ, Nevin has been in our home several times leading a Bible study. Why don't we take the cotton bag containing the four glass specimens to his place of employment and ask him to enlighten us as to the identity and purpose of the glass discs."

"That's a good suggestion, Howie. Pick me up here at home and we'll drive to the Optical Company this afternoon."

Thirty minutes later the detectives stood at the reception desk making an oral plea to talk to the scientist. Miss Witherspoon looked askance at the detectives a full two minutes trying to decide whether to call security police or Dr. McWhimple.

Finally she reached for the phone, tapped a few buttons on the pad, turned her chair to face the wall and in a low voice said, "Err, Doctor, there are two young men with white eyebrows standing in front of my desk. They would like to talk with you for a few minutes. They could be a couple of 'nuts' loose from some asylum or clowns on vacation from the circus..... Yes, and possibly workmen at the local flour mill. Their faces and hair have a white dusting and ...... alright, I'll send them to the conference room."

The receptionist frowned, pointed to her right and said, "He'll meet both of you in the conference room, down that hall, second door on your left. He is on his lunch break so he may may bring his brown bag with him."

"Thank you, Miss Witheredspoon, I mean Witherspoon," stuttered Howie.

As the detectives left her desk and walked toward the designated room she muttered softly, "Now I have something very odd to share with the ladies in the break room."

Five minutes later a short thin man clad in a white frock marched stiffly into the conference room, looked around, recognized Howie and greeted both detectives warmly. Howie introduced Sam and they retired to seats around the large oval-shaped table. A large glass prism perched on a twelve-inch wood pedestal dominated the table top as a centerpiece display of a product created by The Marston Optical Company.

During the next twenty minutes the detectives explained the background and the reason behind their request for the discussion with the scientist.

Howie handed the cotton flour bag containing the four glass discs to Nevin with the comment, "This cotton bag contains the glass discs we found in flour sacks piled on the floor of the Prudely mansion tower."

After another few seconds, Dr. Nevin McWhimple wiped his mouth with a brown paper napkin, readjusted his large, plastic-framed glasses and took one of the pieces of glass out of the flour sack and held it up close to his face.

Finally, after examining the surfaces and edge of the object he pursed his lips and spoke. "Howie and Sam, you have made an amazing discovery. In my hand I am holding a lens we here at The Marston Optical Company developed and produced during the recent war.....see, our company logo is infused with black letters in miniature on the edge."

"Yes, I hadn't noticed those marks," whispered Sam, holding the lens up closer to his eyes.

"This lens," continued Nevin, "manufactured to fit into the periscope of submarines is a product of our firm. If you can remain here for a few more minutes I will share with you some history that pertains to this lens."

An hour later the trio stood up. The two detectives were speechless. Extending their hands they commented, "We will need to share this information with Sheriff Neverfine and his cabinet of associates."

"You may repeat my commentary at the cabinet meeting. Tell your group the discussion is privileged to remain within that setting. I know the war has been over for approximately three years. However,

subversive elements may still be hanging around in the shadows.....
All of our work is now and always has been classified and destined
for the submarines commissioned by the The United States Navy and
the naval fleets of our allies. Our superior quality lenses are being
installed in the periscopes of our most modern submarines."

"Thank you, Nevin, for your cordial commentary regarding the
lenses. We appreciate you utilizing your lunch break to chat with us."

Sam and Howie walked out of the company lobby and into the
sunshine. Walking slowly to their red truck, Howie murmured, "Sam,
a critical component of our navy's submarine fleet is manufactured
right here in Marston, Indiana."

"You're right, and we almost missed the clue, the glass lenses
fabricated for submarine periscopes stuffed inside the marked sacks
of **M**illsaap flour with the darkened right leg of the letter **M**."

"Now, Sam, who do you think planted the four lenses in the
marked sacks of flour?"

"I don't have a clue. However, since we found the lenses stuffed
into sacks of flour milled at The Millsaap Mill we should make
another visit to that establishment, this time at night."

"Sam, we have a real mystery staring right at us. I thought
with the demise of Red Fox our detective work would ease off. But
now I believe we are knee-deep in another mind-jarring, baffling
investigation."

"The next meeting of the sheriff's cabinet will be a 'dilly'."

"Yeah, I can hardly wait."

# Chapter 10

D ETECTIVES HOWIE AND SAM ARRIVED at their office early the
next morning. They bent over their desks writing their reports
they would present orally at the upcoming sheriff's cabinet meeting
later that day.

"Sam, I think my summary of our examination of the flour sacks
that were strewn on the tower floor is complete at least to the extent
of my memory. Have you finished your written review of our visit
with Dr. Nevin McWhimple at the Marston Optical Company?"

"Yeah, but I'm not sure I have included all the necessary details
he related to us. However, my report will inform the cabinet members
of the main results of our conversation with the optical expert
yesterday."

Looking up at the clock Sam suggested, "Since the cabinet
meeting convenes at 2 o'clock this afternoon we have time this
morning to revisit the tower. No doubt Spade has removed the human
form from the stool and we can look through the telescope to see the
view that interested The TatterBitty."

"I'm not sure we should reenter the tower with that purpose in mind. The sheriff stipulated our search should include the bags of flour, not the area at the top of the tower."

"We'll make the assumption that his order included the entire internal structure including the glassed-in windows in the turret at the top.....come on, Howie, let's go."

Arriving at the Prudely mansion thirty minutes later the detectives smiled at the bear's face and marched through the entry door to the tower floor. Quickly mounting the spiral staircase to the top they again marveled at the panoramic view before them. "Sam, the stool where The TatterBitty sat is now empty."

"Spade and his helpers deserve a medal for the delicate and sensitive task of carrying the TatterBitty's corpse down the squeaky, rusty spiral stairs," observed Howie.

"Go ahead, Howie; sit on the stool, put your face up against the telescope and tell me what you see."

Slowly and carefully, Howie mounted the rusted metal stool, wiped the surface of the telescope lens with his handkerchief, moved his eye close to the eyepiece of the telescope and squinted.

"Sam, I can see clearly the cupola at the top of the Millsaap Flour Mill. This telescope seems to be locked in the correct position for viewing that structure."

"Can you see the windows in the cupola?"

"Yes, and I can see the blind that you lowered yesterday over the center window....Sam, take my place on this stool and tell me what you see."

Adjusting his backside on the metal stool Sam moved his face up against the telescope eyepiece. After a long minute he looked down and said in a low voice, "Howie, I see the blind pulled down over the center window. And, someone has cut small holes in the blind, a series of round dots and several longer, narrow spaces. Even in this bright sunlight the holes seem to be black openings cut into the blind material. There must be a sheet of black paper pasted to the back of the blind. Using your notepad jot down my descriptions of the sequences of holes as I describe them to you."

"I'm ready, go ahead; What do you see?"

"First, a group of three dots in a row; then, a sequence of three dashes; and, finally three more dots arranged in a line. What could all those series of holes grouped into three sequences mean?"

"I have no idea. Let's get back to our office and write up a summary of your observations."

Descending the stairs as quickly as possible Sam and Howie started to quickly leave the Prudely mansion. As they bolted toward the tower door Sam stumbled over the old, inverted, rusted, metal wash tub. With his arms flailing about he fell headlong to the concrete floor amidst another pile of flour sacks.

As he stood up he yelled, "Howie, look at that--- hidden under that old tub is an old Farnsworth table radio and another Millsaap flour sack with the darkened **M** letter. We'll take the sack back to our office and cut it open later. We may find another glass lens inside."

As the detectives quietly drove back to their office Howie remarked, "Yes, in a short time we will be able to share with the sheriff's cabinet members some very strange and sinister items and events."

# Chapter 11

O N THAT WEDNESDAY AFTERNOON, OCTOBER 27th, Sheriff Neverfine experienced mixed emotions. He looked at today's date circled in red ink on his desk calendar. During the last few days he had dropped a few hints at home and around the jail office that this date coincided with his 50th birthday....he smiled broadly. No doubt, Clara, his lovely wife would bake his favorite indulgence, a chocolate fudge cake, arranged in three thick layers.

She would top each layer of the cake with a thick covering of fudge frosting. Then, during that enchanted, romantic evening she would present the culinary masterpiece to him with a smile, pomp and soft music. Fifty candles inserted in the top layer would light up the dining room as he personally touched a long lighted match to each one.

Then his thoughts jolted to the present time. Sitting at his desk and nibbling on a ham sandwich brought in earlier that day by Snooper, he stared at the agenda for the cabinet meeting scheduled to begin in a few minutes. His countenance changed to a serious mode.

Hopefully, his cabinet members would bring closure to several investigations he had ordered during the previous meeting. "But," he muttered out loud, "would the discussion bring additional issues to light necessitating additional official inquiries?"

He frowned, inhaled deeply, grabbed his favorite coffee mug and walked heavily to the conference room. The cabinet members smiled, stood up and with uneven harmony bellowed out, 'Happy Birthday to You, Sheriff' Neverfine', three times. The sheriff, momentarily nonplussed finally smiled and mumbled with a faint hint of modesty, "Thanks, I didn't think anyone would remember the date for my birthday. Now, let's get serious. We have some important agenda items on our schedule today."

After visually scanning the day's agenda again, the sheriff stated, "The discussion during our last meeting generated a desire for further investigation of several areas...We needed more data and information to suggest further action and direction."

After glancing around the table to make sure everyone remained awake he stated, "We will hear the results of these inquiries today. Therefore our first agenda item is a report by Sam and Howie summarizing their recent inspection trip to the Millsaap Flour Mill.... Okay, detectives, you're on....and make it brief."

As Howie distributed a one-page outline to the members he began his discussion of the contents. "As you will note, Sam, Inspector Snooper, Frank Overbaring and I visited The Millsaap Flour Mill last Friday."

Glancing at the inspector, Howie continued, "Inspector Snooper had called Mr. Silas Canbee, the manager of the mill to make arrangements for our visit. Snoop, share with this group your overall impressions of that visit."

The inspector cleared his throat, scanned his notes and after a long nervous bout of fake coughing to alleviate an imaginary tickling sensation in his throat he began, "We arrived at the mill, located on the east bank of the Mississinewa River at 9 o'clock, October 29th, a sunny day. Mr. Canbee received us cordially. He led our group to a small room where we could witness the huge, rotating water wheel powering the grinding mechanism and other mechanics necessary for the milling process. Then he led us on a tour of the mill."

"Is the mill busy? Are the services offered by the mill in demand?" asked the sheriff.

"Yes, the mill operates six days a week with a work force of four men during the day and two at night. On the day of our visit two farmers waited for the workers to unload their trucks loaded with sacks of wheat."

"Inspector, did you notice anything suspicious while touring the plant?" asked Captain Firmly.

"Not until we climbed to the top of the structure and entered the cupola."

"Be brief, Snoop. Finish up your report. We have other items to discuss," directed the sheriff as he doodled aimlessly and nervously on the agenda page.

"Entering the cupola on the fourth floor of the mill we could see out over most of the houses and other buildings in Marston......But, two items in the cupola caught our attention. Sam, tell the group about the window shades and the instrument in the box."

Clearing his throat, Sam began, " Every window in the cupola has a rolled-up shade or blind at the top. That feature is not unusual since customers can relax in this area while waiting for their wheat or corn to be milled. When lowered, the blinds reduce the heat in the room on summer days. However, we noticed an odd feature on at least one blind. Small round and rectangular holes had been cut out of the material."

"Very interesting, Sam. So you discovered a weathered blind with holes. Now, tell us about the box you noticed on the floor of the room?" prodded the sheriff.

"Our discovery of the box surprised Mr. Canbee who seldom finds it necessary to climb the steps up to the cupola. He scooted the container to the center of the floor. Dropping to his knees he untied the cord binding the box and forced off the lid."

Sam hesitated to increase the sheriff"'s impatience, then continued. "We all crowded around and gawked as Silas lifted a metal object out of the box. We had discovered some kind of instrument. The gadget comprised a lens on the end of a metal tube about six inches in diameter. Everyone expressed doubt as to the purpose of such a gadget. Mr. Overbaring snapped photos of the box and the instrument."

Continuing, Sam informed the cabinet members, "Then yesterday Captain Firmly, Howie and I visited with Frank Overbaring at *The Marston Tribune* offices. We wanted to view the close-up image of the instrument on the developed photo taken at the Millsaap Flour Mill. Captain, tell our cabinet members your analysis of the photo."

"Thank you, Sam. Yes, being a former U. S. Navy man I immediately identified the instrument as a signal lamp used during the recent war. This lamp, commonly referred to as a 'Morse lamp', is a visual signaling device, typically using Morse Code. The instrument found at The Millsaap Flour Mill is hand-held. A concave mirror is tilted by trigger action to focus the light into pulses that can be seen and interpreted by a person viewing the light pulses."

"Possibly someone positioned in the cupola at the mill would aim the light at the tower of the Prudely Mansion. Then by opening and closing the shutter over the lamp, that person could send flashes of light to spell out messages in Morse Code," added Captain Firmly.

"Thank you, Detectives Sam and Howie, Inspector Snooper and Captain Firmly for information concerning your visit to and inspection of the Millsaap Flour Mill. We appreciate your making available to each member of this cabinet a copy of your report. Also, Captain Firmly, thank you for analyzing the photos taken by Frank Overbaring."

"Now, Sam and Howie, before our next meeting continue your investigation to determine why a signal lamp would be stored in a room on the top floor of The Millsaap Flour Mill, a building that processes wheat into flour and corn into meal. This meeting is adjourned." The sheriff gathered his papers and stood up anxious to visit the table supporting the coffee urn and doughnuts.

"Oh, sheriff, Howie and I forgot to mention one additional outcome of our last trip to explore the tower at the Prudely mansion."

"Well, go ahead and make it quick."

"After we had investigated the area at the top of the tower, including the stool used by The Tatterbitty, we decided to leave the tower."

"Yeah, what new developments do you want to disclose?" encouraged the sheriff, coughing loudly.

"We scurried down the metal, spiral staircase to vacate the tower."

"Of course you climbed down the stairs. That's the only means of returning to the floor level. Why are you bothering us with such trivia?" asked the sheriff, standing up.

"As I scrambled toward the 'bear-faced' door I tripped over an old rusted, discarded laundry tub."

"I don't see that you suffered any injury from your fall."

"Right, but look at this scrap of paper we found hidden inside a flour sack secreted under the laundry tub."

"Sam, I'm not interested right now in hearing about one more flour sack. Keep the sack and the scrap of paper in your office. Maybe we'll open and consider it at a future cabinet meeting."

The sheriff made eye contact with each cabinet member, shook his head and declared, "This investigation is driving me crazy. Each day we uncover new clues that demand our attention. Let's take a 30 minute break. When you return we will hear a report by Spade Digger and Captain Firmly. Now if you will excuse me I need to make a run to the bathroom."

As the members moved toward the refreshment table they smiled as they heard the sounds of the sheriff's heavy shoes clomping in rapid sequence toward the rear of the jail.

# Chapter 12

WHEN ALL THE CABINET MEMBERS had returned to the conference room with re-filled coffee mugs Sheriff Neverfine coughed, thumped his coffee mug on the table top, swabbed his mouth with a handful of wrinkled, tan paper towels and said in a rather loud commanding voice, "Alright, let's get down to business. Spade, share with our group your process of removal and possible identification of the two forms we have labeled corpses that our cabinet members recently discovered in the tower of the Prudely mansion."

Turning to face the county's chief lawman the mortician rather pointedly and brusquely spoke. "Sheriff, no one around this table can realize or even imagine the difficulties we faced in fulfilling that assignment."

Rather chagrined, the sheriff squirmed about on his chair and tried to reassure the mortician. Pointing his just-sharpened lead pencil at the mortician he replied, "Mr. Digger, perhaps none of us sitting here in this room or the citizens in Marston can have full empathy or appreciation for you as you fulfill the responsibilities of your chosen profession. Let me assure you that you have our complete emotional and physical support; Please proceed."

"Thank you, Sheriff. Now to my report. Captain Firmly and two of my regular, on-call helpers, arrived at the Prudely Mansion with ropes, pulleys, a foldaway cot with aluminum frame, the type used by emergency medical personnel, and an electric winch."

"With all that equipment and assistance you probably completed the removal of the bodies in a short time," implied Inspector Snooper with a slight smirk.

Glaring at Snooper, Spade straightened his posture and caressed a miniature coffin attached to a gold chain stretched across the front of his black vest. Adjusting and smoothing his recently laundered, black coat he ignored the inspector's comment and continued. "The removal of the small corpse stuffed inside the Millsaap Flour Mill sack required only identification of the correct sack. We transported those remains to my mortuary. I'll provide more information about our examination of that body later in my presentation."

Spade reached for a glass tumbler half full of water, drained a large quantity into his mouth and gargled loudly. Slightly embarrassed he glanced around at the frowns on the expectant faces of the members and added, "The removal of The TatterBitty from the tower proved to be a huge challenge."

The members waited expectantly. The stuffy humid air in the room caused everyone to nervously squirm about on their chairs and mop their brows. The mortician added, "Since we couldn't remove the curved rectangular windows at the top to lower the body to the ground outside the tower wall using the folding cot and the winch"........He reached for the water tumbler again and slurped.

"Spade, we don't have all afternoon. Did you remove The TatterBitty from the tower or not?" demanded the sheriff, obviously exasperated.

"Yes, yes, I'm getting to the devised method we cleverly used to lower The TatterBitty...Captain Firmly gently removed the body from the stool, placed the form over his right shoulder and step by step he eased it down the spiral staircase. The TatterBitty is now a resident at my mortuary in a refrigerated drawer immediately under that of the 'flour bag body'."

Howie spoke up. "Thank you, Spade, for completing the sensitive assigned task of removing the two bodies. Now, you earlier stated you possess additional information about the flour sack body. Please elaborate."

"Yes, Dr. Stephen Younger, a pediatrician at the Children's Hospital in Indianapolis, assisted me at my mortuary with the difficult task of examining the flour sack body. The jumbled, disjointed and misplaced bones entailed a lengthy and difficult process of reconstruction. We finally reassembled the skeleton, covered with rather small bits of dried body parts and flakes of discolored skin. Our findings are temporary, incomplete and inconclusive."

The sheriff stood up and shouted, "Alright, Spade, spit it out! Tell us now the results of your examination of the 'flour sack body'." He then sat down with an audible 'thump'.

"Our tentative conclusion is the dead remains in question are that of a young male perhaps fifteen years old."

"Spade, are you suggesting the body of a dead teen-ager could be stuffed into a fifty pound flour sack?" spouted Sam, frowning.

"Yes; judging from the size and length of the skeletal bones the male possessed a very small stature, possibly born a dwarf."

The sheriff quietly jotted notes on the back of the agenda sheet. He mused, "What relationship would a dwarf have with the former residents of the Prudely mansion?"

Then he looked up and asked, "Now, Spade, what information can you share with this group concerning The TatterBitty?"

"The TatterBitty is a female, approximately 10-12 years old, dead perhaps 5-7 years. The garment she is wearing at the time of our discovery displays long, narrow ribbons of material cut from used, colorful, cotton flour sacks----and, the garment fragments seem to have been fabricated from large Millsaap Flour Mill sacks. Someone cut the sacks into strips, dyed them with various vivid colors, then hand-printed the strips with grotesque stick figures depicting animals and people. Then the ribbons of material, sewed together emerged as a colorful garment worn by The TatterBitty."

After a long silence the sheriff coughed lightly and asked, "Spade, do you or any of your colleagues know the identity of either The TatterBitty or the flour sack body? And, do you have a clue as to why the dead bodies ended up inside the tower of the Prudely mansion?"

"No, sheriff, we have no clue as to where The Tatterbitty or the flour sack body died. They may have died elsewhere and their bodies transferred to the tower. That determination and the answers to your questions are the responsibility of you and the members of this cabinet."

"As to the true identity of the TatterBitty and the flour sack bodies, the only possible indications resulting from our examination are metal bracelets found fastened around the wrist bones of the right arm of each body."

The sheriff stood up and demanded, " Well, did the bracelets exhibit any identifying marks?"

"Yes. The bracelet dangling on the wrist bones of the flour sack skeleton has the engraved initials J. A. P.; the bracelet on the wrist of The TatterBitty is inscribed with the initials J. O. P."

"Thank you, Spade, for all your professional efforts and today's succinct presentation. We have many hours of work ahead of us...... Sam and Howie, I want to see you in my office at 8 o' clock this next Monday morning. This meeting is adjourned."

# *Chapter 13*

A FTER A RESTFUL WEEKEND WITH their spouses that included hearing a stirring sermon preached by Reverend Rob Kneel at the local Methodist Church and picnicing with their spouses at Matter Park, Sam and Howie felt ready to face the sheriff.

They locked their office door on that Monday, scampered across 3rd Street and entered the Gurant County Jail.

Sheriff Neverfine, Inspector Snooper and Spade Digger waited for them in the conference room. "Good morning, Howie and Sam," offered the sheriff. Snooper nodded his head as he continued to examine his fingernails. Spade raised his right hand slightly in greeting.

"Good day, Sheriff, Spade and Inspector Snooper," replied Howie, as the detectives found chairs and sat down near the sheriff.

"You asked for some conference time with us this morning. What's up?" asked Sam, glancing at the sheriff while opening a notebook, pencil in hand.

"The Inspector, Spade and I wanted to talk with you both and discuss the appropriate steps to fulfill our next request."

"And what is that request, Sheriff?" asked Howie, his eyebrows raised.

"We, as chief lawmen for this county, would like for you two detectives as a team, to complete a clandestine night-time visit to the Millsaap Flour Mill," directed the sheriff.

Before the detectives could respond he added, "At the cabinet meeting last week, Captain Firmly indicated a weathered box found on the floor of the cupola of the mill contained a signal lamp. The Inspector and I want you two detectives to pursue and examine the events surrounding that discovery; determine the purpose for that signal lamp and why it is located in the cupola of the Millsaap Flour Mill."

"Howie and I think we know the purpose of the signal lamp."

"You do! Well, let's have it."

"A few days ago, without your express permission, Howie and I completed another visit to the Prudely house, with the specific purpose of exploring the tower."

"I recall your previous trip included your intention to examine the flour inside the sacks strewn about the tower floor," recalled Snooper.

"During this visit we climbed the spiral staircase and discovered The TatterBitty had been removed by Spade Digger and Captain Firmly."

"Yes, if you will remember, Sam, the members of this cabinet requested that action, Now, continue. What is your point?"

"The empty metal stool, previously occupied by The TatterBitty, invited me to sit on it and view the scene as seen by that figure clad in the colorful tattered rags as she looked through the telescope."

"Did you see anything beside the roof tops of houses?"

"Yes, the telescope is mounted on a tripod with the direction fixed toward the Millsaap Flour Mill. When I focused on the cupola I noticed one of the blinds had been lowered."

"So you looked at a window blind, probably lowered by a Mill customer to reduce the temperature inside the area. Why are you taking our time telling us about a window blind?" demanded the sheriff, rather gruffly.

Sam inhaled and began. "Evidently a black sheet of some material has been pasted to the back side of the blind. Thus I could visualize several round and many narrow rectangular pieces of blind had been cut out of the fabric."

"The blind probably ripped when lowered. Those blinds must be years old. You surely don't think a ragged old window blind influences our discussion today," demanded the sheriff as he figeted and frowned.

"Perhaps the holes in the blind are important, Sheriff. When I focused on the black areas three sequences of dots and dashes appeared."

Inspector Snooper's eyes opened wide. He stopped doodling on the puzzle page of the *Marston Tribune* and became alert focusing on the detective's comments.

The sheriff leaned forward, his chin supported by a cupped hand and burly forearm and said, "Sam, you have lost me. Explain in plain English what you viewed through the telescope."

"Howie, share with the sheriff and Inspector Snooper the three sequences of holes and what they may indicate."

"Err, Yes....in the first sequence, three circular dots are apparent; then a second series includes three longer rectangular bars; the third and final group consists of three circular dots."

"Make your presentation easy for me, Howie," ordered the sheriff, moping his brow. "What did you conclude about the holes you observed in the blind at the cupola?"

"Our research of signaling using Morse Code indicates the three sequences of holes express an S. O. S."

After a few minutes of quiet, the inspector looked at the detectives and asked, "Are you suggesting that someone at the Mill wanted to send this request for help to a person in the tower at the Prudely home?"

"Yes, someone at the Millsaap Mill has been desperate for help and displayed the International code signal of extreme distress. That person hoped someone at the Prudely tower would answer by coming to their aid," explained Sam.

"I'm with you, Sam, but who at the tower could answer?" inquired Inspector Snooper.

"Yes," agreed Spade. "Since the stool behind the telescope at the tower is now vacant, no one is available to answer or respond to the S. O. S."

"However," responded Sam, "the sender of signals at the mill may not have been aware of recent happenings at the tower. That person assumed a person sat at the telescope available to receive the message."

Suddenly the sheriff stood up and declared, "We are wasting time. Detectives Sam and Howie, make your second visit to the Millsaap Flour Mill tonight. Come back to this cabinet with answers to our questions...and you both should carry your 38's........Inspector Snooper, please remain for a few minutes. You indicated a desire to discuss with me an interesting phone call you received from Dr. Nevin McWhimple."

That night at eleven o'clock, Sam and Howie, wearing soft-soled shoes and dark outer clothing stood on the driveway near the platform used by local farmers and mill employees to off load their sacks of wheat or corn at the Millsaap Flour Mill. Sam had parked their red pick-up truck two blocks away on a side street. He looked up, punched Howie on the arm, pointed and said in a low voice, "There is someone up in the cupola. See those lights bouncing around."

"Yeah, that's good news. The two night workers must be up there, leaving the lower three floors void of people. Also, the grinding mechanism is idle so this area is very quiet.....Let's see if we can enter the mill. Since the water wheel is stable maybe we can slide through the space between the wood spokes and over the top of the gear wheel and the grindstones."

After several minutes of crawling through the spaces between the flat wood paddles of the water wheel the detectives dropped to the lower level of the mill. Howie brushed the moist dirt and debris from his overalls and softly suggested, "Here we are, Sam, standing in the basement where the flour is bagged. How can we move up to the cupola without the benefit of the hoist that depends on the power of the moving water wheel?"

"There has to be a series of steps to the top of the mill for safety reasons in case of fire or if the hoist breaks down....Yes, over there next to that wall," suggested Sam pointing to one side of the room.

Quietly the detectives soft-shoed up narrow wood steps to the top floor and approached the door to the cupola. They could hear subdued voices coming from the interior of the room. As they crept closer to an open door the conversation within the cupola became audible. The detectives stood quietly and listened intently.

"Horst, when I looked through our portable telescope in the direction of the tower the place appeared dark."

"Yah, and we haven't received an answer to our S. O. S. plea. I'm worried. During his last trip to the flour mill Mr. McWhimple assured us he could help us leave this town at the appropriate, agreed-upon time."

"He has been very responsive, replying to our urgent messages transmitted by signal lamp over the past several months and years."

"That's right. Remember, a young girl also sent us messages from the tower using the signal lamp. Maybe she can help us now."

"Yah, I remember the young girl, Horst. She identified herself as a ten year old but I have forgotten her name."

"Then Ovid Prudely forced some drugged job applicants to transmit messages before they traveled by truck to Cincinnati, Ohio, where I understand they boarded a river boat en route to South America."

"Yah; also, Red Fox coerced a dwarf who had been living at the mansion for years to send us many signals. He could hardly see through the telescope because he wasn't tall enough to reach the eyepiece. I think he had to sit on a couple of pillows."

"I remember the dwarf signalled that Red Fox forced him to transmit messages to the flour mill. Do you remember the night he talked about the chemical formula he developed for a compound he labeled BrainX? He asked if we could help him take the formula to some safe place such as South America or Germany. He told us BrainX could make ordinary people like us become obedient slaves, responding only to the will of a master such as Red Fox."

"But now that information is useless because Red Fox is dead..... Wait a minute, Gerhard. Maybe we could benefit by producing and promoting BrainX. We could inject BrainX into the veins of a subject and give that person the orders to fulfill our wishes and follow our directions."

"Put that idea in your rear pocket, Horst. Our immediate need is to get out of this town and return to Germany, our homeland."

"Well fortunately, as of tonight, we will not need to send any more distress messages by signal lamps. Mr. McWhimple informed us yesterday by phone he is coming here tonight in a rowboat between midnight and two o' clock. We will then vacate this flour mill, walk to the river, step in a rowboat and bid this flour mill and the United States a final goodbye."

"If our escape is successful Mr. McWhimple's name will be McAble, and he will not only show us how to vacate Marston and leave this country but he will also provide the funds for our trip. Gerhard, we will be back in Germany in one week." Both men smiled broadly.

Suddenly, Gerhard held up one hand and placed a finger over his mouth. "Horst," he whispered wide-eyed, "I'm afraid we have a visitor....Someone just sneezed outside that door."

"Mr. McWhimple is not due until after midnight. We may have a vagrant wanting to spend the night at the vacant flour mill....we endured two of those rascals last week."

"I'll escort the unwelcome intruder down the steps and kick him out over the sluice trough. Perhaps a good dousing in the river will teach him that this building is off limits to free-loaders."

"Why are you woried about some vagrants, Gerhard? After tonight we won't have to worry about strangers."

"Yeah, you're right. But, we don't want any strangers around tonight to possibly spoil our plans to vacate this mill."

"Hand me that ball bat we use to kill rats, Gerhard. I'll get rid of that intruder in a hurry."

# Chapter 14

S AM WIPED HIS NOSE ON his shirt sleeve and motioned for Howie to follow. He whispered, "I felt that sneeze coming on but couldn't muffle it. I'm sure the persons inside the cupola heard the noise."

The detectives began a furious mad scramble down the treacherous wood steps. As they passed the second floor, Howie, stepping heavily, broke through a cracked wood step. He toppled forward and fell against Sam. Both detectives tumbled down to the first floor and landed next to the grain hopper located just above the 'runner', the grinding stone.

Howie, landing on top of Sam struggled to his feet and reached for Sam's belt to help him to stand up. Both detectives, disoriented in the murky darkness, waddled about trying to locate the exit door to Mr. Canbee's office. Sam tripped and fell headlong on top of the grinding stone.

Horst and Gerhard following close behind, stumbled down the same narrow steps and fell in a heap on the ground floor. Gerhard, without a word, gestered to Horst as he grabbed and yanked down on the wood lever controlling the sluice gate. Immediately water rushed forward and splashed against the paddles on the water wheel causing it to rotate. Horst opened the slide allowing grain to flow from the hopper onto the grinding stone.

Suddenly Sam began to rotate on top of the grindstone. He yelled, "Howie, they have opened the sluice gate! The water wheel is turning and my shirt sleeve is caught under the turning grindstone! I'm being dragged around in circles!"

Howie shouted, "I'm trying to close the sluice gate, Sam! It seems to be stuck open! Don't let your head get caught in the gear wheel! I'll crawl out and try to close the sluice gate with my foot!"

As Howie crawled out over the wood cross beams that stabilized the water wheel his shoe slipped and became entangled with the outer part of the rotating water wheel. Now his entire body began to flail about as he rotated in a circular vertical path, his foot lodged between two paddles of the water wheel.

Sam, rotating on the grinding stone and Howie, his foot caught in the water wheel found themselves in an extremely dangerous and helpless quandry. Howie, dunked under the surface of the river water during each rotation, held his breath until the wheel rotated enough for him to beathe again.

Meanwhile, Horst and Gerhard stood by staring and smiling, confident they had stopped any action that would interfere with their planned exit from the mill, guided by Mr. McWhimple.

Suddenly they heard a shrill whistle coming from across the river. Staring across the waters of the Mississinewa river they noticed a blinking light. "Horst," yelled Gerhard, "that's the signal from McWhimple....He's over there on the opposite river bank. There's enough moonlight for us to see his silloute. He's standing up in the rowboat and waving his arms."

"Good; Come on, Gerhard, let's run quickly downstream on the river shore. We'll hide in that grove of trees and wait for McWhimple."

"He has arrived just like he promised. We will be in good hands. He will assist us on our journey home to Germany."

"Can he see us here on this side?" asked Gerhard. "This area is very dark with no moonlight or street lights. I hope he can spot us here under these trees. I'm glad McWhimple is rowing the boat to this side of the river. I don't think I could swim across...the current is too brisk."

"Yeah, wave your arms and yell like crazy, Gerhard. He should be able to hear you since your voice sounds like a bull bellowing."

"Yah," said Horst in a heavy whisper a few minutes later, "I think he can see us. He is sitting down in the boat and now he's beginning to row the craft faster in this direction."

———————◆◆◆◆◆———————

A half hour earlier, Sheriff Neverfine had steered his cruiser close to the entry door to the mill. As he opened the cruiser door he could hear tormented cries for help coming from the rotating water wheel.

Running forward he quickly realized someone seemed to be in a precarious situation. A person with arms and legs flailing about seemed to be attached to the outer rim of the water wheel. As the wheel turned the figure disappeared under the moving river water with each rotation ......Yes, now he recognized Howie's anguished voice. As he ran toward the area he could see the detective, his arms and legs floundering about, rotating around and around, his left foot and pant leg caught on a paddle of the water wheel.

Howie caught a glimpse of the sheriff and yelled, "Sheriff, close the sluice gate!.... When the water stops flowing this water wheel will stop turning!"

The sheriff climbed up on the framework supporting the moving water wheel and located the appropriate lever. Seizing it he shoved it forward. Quickly the flow of rushing water stopped and the water wheel slowed to a groaning, squeaking stop.

In turn the grindstone also stopped rotating. Sam yelled, "Sheriff, use your jack knife and cut off my right shirt sleeve. Then I can climb down off this grinding wheel."

Sam and Sheriff Neverfine then managed to free Howie's right shoe and foot from the water wheel. The sheriff ordered, "Now, Sam and Howie, sit down here out of sight in the shadow of the mill. We will soon have visitors coming ashore in a rowboat."

Several minutes later Sheriff Neverfine, Sam and Howie stood in the dark shadow of the mill staring at a rowboat moving closer to the eastern shore.

As the rowboat touched the shore Horst and Gerhard splashed out and jumped in the boat.

To everyone's surprise Sheriff Neverfine suddenly appeared, grabbed the attached rope and pulled the craft up further on the muddy river bank.

"What's this lying in the bottom of the boat?" yelled Horst, oblivious to the sheriff's presence. Staring down toward his shoes he instinctively reached down and touched the still form.

"It's a body!" he screamed, as he reached down and turned the head face up. "Gerhard, it's Dr. McWhimple!"

"Yes, your personal guide to show you the way to your home in Germany is temporarily incapacitated," suggested the man who released his grip on the oars and stood up.

"Then, who are you?" gasped Horst, his eyes wide open.

"People around here call me Inspector Snooper. As you will notice my special police model '38 is pointed at your mid-section.... Now, step out of this craft and lie face down on the muddy river bank. I have a very nervous trigger finger. If this weapon discharges each of you will experience extreme pain. Your innards will gush out of your body leaving a bleeding, gaping hole in your mid-section."

Their mouths gaping open, Gerhard and Horst meekly and obediently obeyed the Inspector's directions. Snooper quickly snapped handcuffs on the wrists of both Horst and Gerrhard linking them together.

# *Chapter 15*

ASSUMING COMMAND THE SHERIFF SHOUTED, "Good work, Snooper. The scheme we devised to capture the two mill workers worked to perfection. The mysterious telephone conversation you had with Dr. McWhimple enabled us to devise this plan to capture the two German mill workers...Now help me place our two prisoners, handcuffed together, in the rear of my cruiser."

The sheriff glanced at the two detectives and ordered, "Sam and Howie, go home and get some sleep. My cabinet will meet tomorrow at noon. Our agenda is loaded...plan to spend the afternoon with us at the jail."

Sam and Howie looked at each other rather dumb founded. Sam leaned over and mumured, "What agenda topics and the resulting discussion could possibly consume the entire afternoon hours? Well, we will find out tomorrow. Let's follow the sheriff's order, Howie. We need some down time."

The next day a few minutes after the clock on top of the County Court House belted out twelve tones the conference room at the jail became a flurry of activity amid loud chattering voices. As the cabinet members entered they stared at the side table with amazement. Numerous large containers laden with colorful food items created enticing aromas and a feast for the eyes of the hungry cabinet members and guests.

Promply at one o'clock, Sheriff Neverfine, in a rather boisterous manner, barged into the room leading two guests, both strangers to the cabinet members. Suddenly the room quieted and eyes widened as everyone gaped at the guests. As usual, the sheriff assumed leadership and announced loudly, "Good afternoon everyone. I would like for you to meet our two guests. On my left," smiled the sheriff as he stepped closer to the young woman and loudly said, "this young lady, a resident of Marston her entire life, lives on Appalling Street next to the Prudely house. Her name is Miss Gladys Fedders....and, on my right is retired Admiral Theodore Radar of the U. S. Navy. They both will join us in our discussion today after we enjoy the sumpuous vittles prepared by my lovely wife, Clara, and Zsofia, our cook at the jail. Thank you, ladies, for preparing and delivering this meal to the conference room.....now, Sam, please lead us in prayer."

Sam stepped forward, bowed his head and prayed; "Lord, we pause to give thanks for the food prepared for our well-being. Each day you provide for our basic physical and spiritual needs and for that we give you thanks. Bless each person here and guide our discussion this afternoon. We pray in the name of Jesus the Christ. Amen."

The sheriff's booming voice emerged; "Now, please allow our guests to proceed through the food line first. We will convene our cabinet meeting at 2 o'clock."

\* \* \*

The time passed quickly. The atmosphere in the conference room, punctuated with loud conversation, uproarious laughter, back-slapping and numerous trips to the food table, resembled an old fashioned rural 'threshing ring' dinner. Finally at 2 o'clock the sheriff's booming voice quieted the group. After thanking Clara Morhusky Neverfine and Zsofia, the jail cook again for preparing the meal he announced the opening of the business portion of the meeting by thumping his coffee mug on the conference table top.

"Cabinet members," he intoned, "thank you for taking another afternoon of your valuable time to help bring closure to some very perplexing local issues dealing with law enforcement."

After glancing around the table and making eye contact with everyone the sheriff announced loudly, "It is my privilege to present our two guests who will share information for our knowledge and discussion. Each of the two guests deserves privacy of information regarding their conversation with us today."

The cabinet members, burping and draining the final sip from their cups of coffee, settled on their chairs now ready and anxious for an extended time of listening and discussion.

"Our first guest," declared the sheriff, "Admiral Theodore Radar, has another obligation this afternoon. His daughter will be married at the local Methodist Church, the ceremony to be conducted by our distinguished minister, Reverend Rob Kneel. Therefore, the admiral asked to be number one on our agenda. Admiral, share with this group what you have told me regarding the periscope lenses produced by the Marston Optical Company."

"Thank you, Sheriff Neverfine, and good day to you all. My expertise is military intelligence with a specialty in submarine warfare. My service with the United States Navy extended from 1935 through December, 1947."

After making eye contact with each cabinet member he proceeded. "The main reason for my appearance with you today is to highlight and confirm the military service record of Oberleutenant Gregor Mindall, known to you all as Dr. Nevin McWimple, who is currently employed as a laboratory specialist at the Marston Optical Company."

With a determined countenance he continued. "His birth name is Erick Blander. As a commander of a German subnmarine from 1935 till 1943, Blander observed and learned from experience with strategic submarine warfare. As a Commander of U-Boats in the Atlantic Ocean his submarines are credited with sinking many American and British naval and convoy vessels."

The admiral, noticing the frowns of the faces of the members, cleared his throat then remarked, "In June, 1943 the German High Command, recognizing Erick Blander's intelligence and his fluency of the English language, changed the submarine commander's name to Gregor Mindall, promoted him to Oberleutenant and told him he would soon be ordered to serve as an undercover agent in the state of Indiana located in the United States of America."

The cabinet members glanced sideways toward each other, shifting their positions on the cane bottom chairs but remaining alert.

The Admiral continued, "Oberleutenant Mindall, and his fleet of submarines sank many American convoy ships during the early years of the recent war. However, in December, 1943, his submarine, damaged by depth charges dropped from U. S. Navy destroyers, suffered the indignity of being towed to Halifax, Canada, ending Mindall's career of carnage on the high seas as a submarine commander."

"That background is helpful, Admiral, but how does the information relate to the topic of periscope lenses?" asked Captain Firmly, readjusting his position on the cane bottom chair.

"Oberleutenant Gregor Mindall, discouraged and despondent about the carnage his submarines had caused in the Atlantic Ocean, suddenly felt touched by the Holy Spirit in Halifax. He fell on his knees and dedicated his life to follow Jesus the Christ. He approached his American counterpart in Canada. The outcome of his experience in Halifax resulted in Gregor Mindall becoming not only a Christian but also a German undercover agent."

"Continue, Admiral Radar," encouraged Inspector Snooper. "How did Commander Blander end up in Indiana as director of the laboratory at The Marston Optical Company?"

"The Third Reich, desperate for periscope lenses after the R. A. F. bombing of their optical factory in Germany, seemed willing to try subversive techniques to obtain quality lenses for periscopes to be installed in their submarines."

"So," added Admiral Radar, " in 1944 Gregor Mindall assumed the persona of Nevin McWhimple, a German undercover opeator. As a secret agent with a doctorate and expertise in the field of optics, he went underground to serve only one master, The Third Reich."

Captain Firmly broke in and asked, "How did he help the Allies since many of the lenses produced here in Marston ended up in German submarines?"

"Err, yes, that is the pertinent question," answered the Admiral as he turned and gazed out the window for an extended time. Heavy breathing, the only sound in the room, seemed to be quite evident. Finally, he turned and faced the expectant cabinet members sitting upright around the table and spurted, "This information is known only by Dr. Nevin McWhimple, myself and a few high level American military officers."

"The German High Command did not know Dr. McWhimple also served as an agent for the United States military establishment. Unaware of McWhimple's Christian experience and his activity as a U. S. undercover agent, The Third Reich continued to rely upon him for a supply of lenses for their submarines."

Admiral Radar paused, reached for a glass of apple cider and sipped conservatively. Setting the glass down gently he cleared his throat and firmly stated, "Every lens produced here at The Marston Optical Company, destined to be mounted in periscopes of German submarines included a flaw....the molten glass used for the manufacture of the lenses possessed microscopic bubbles and therefore each one contained a defect."

A hush enveloped the conference room as the general added, "Also, the altered curvature of the lens produced for the German submariner peering through the periscope a distorted view of two degrees. The resultant interpretation caused the torpedo to be launched slightly off the desired course, hopefully missing the target."

The members of the cabinet breathed a communal sigh of relief and exchanged brief comments of approval. Then smiles appeared as every person could remember merchant seamen, friends and relatives lost at sea due to German submarine warfare.

Sam broke into the loud conversation by shouting, "Then why did Horst and Gerhard, now our prisoners here at this jail, continue to operate out at The Millsaap Flour Mill? The war ended in 1945!"

"Because, Sam," replied Admiral Radar in an even tone, "they listened only to Red Fox, their mentor and patron, who continued to operate undercover here in Marston. Red Fox, a dedicated Nazi, refused to believe that Germany could suffer defeat. Only after Red Fox died as a result of his fall in a cell in this jail did Horst and Gerhard begin to think for themselves. At that time they decided the time had arrived for their attempt to return to their homeland."

The Admiral added, "I know their loyalty and selfless devotion, their complete dependence upon Red Fox is a mental state that is difficult for all of us to understand; but, thousands upon thousands of German soldiers, sailors, airmen and citizens believed The Third Reich would be victorious and Germany would rule the world for the next one thousand years." Loud conversation erupted among the attendees seated around the table.

"Alright!" blared Sheriff Neverfine, in an attempt to restore order, "let's take a 30 minute break. Please help yourselves to coffee, apple cider and pastries located on the side table. During our next session, Miss Gladys Fedder will share some valuable information with us.....and, thank you, Admiral Theodore Radar, for your valuable presentation. Please convey our best wishes to your daughter as she completes her vows of marriage."

# Chapter 16

SEVERAL MINUTES LATER THE ATTENDEES returned to their seats amid gestures and loud verbal comments about the content of Admiral Radar's presentation. Captain Firmly stroked his chin and remarked, "Our conversations with the admiral during the break proved to be quite informative. Also, at times his comments kindled subtle anger and sad memories."

The captain paused, his eyes became moistened and his jaw vibrated as he attempted to hold back tears. Then he continued, "We remembered our friends and relatives who died as a result of the recent war. Many of those persons now lie at the bottom of the Atlantic Ocean, victims of the torpedoes directed by the German sailors peering through the periscopes fabricated with lenses produced in German factories."

The feelings of the cabinet members became mitigated somewhat by Admiral Radar's comments assuring them that many launched torpedoes missed their mark because of the imperfect lenses produced locally in Marston, Indiana.

Further comments became futile as the sheriff ordered, "Alright, may I please have your attention. We need to hear and consider the comments of our second guest."

After another five minutes of muted but expressive conversation, the cabinet members turned on their chairs and faced the sheriff and the petite woman sitting at his side.

"At this time," offered the sheriff, "it my pleasure to introduce to you Miss Gladys Fedders, who resides at 402 Appalling Street, next door to the Prudely mansion.....Gladys, these men are members of my cabinet, a group of indviduals who offer encouragement and advice for Inspector Snooper and myself. We meet each month or more often if necessary to hear testimony from persons such as yourself who we believe will help us in our collective efforts in law enforcement."

The sheriff sipped more coffee, then continued, "Please be assured your comments shall remain with these individuals, so you can speak freely with confidence of privacy."

Gladys smiled as she glanced around the table and scanned the faces of cabinet members. Without notes or other sources of reference she began to speak. "Thank you, members of Sheriff Neverfine's cabinet, for hearing my comments and remembrances regarding my past involvement with persons inhabiting the mansion at 404 Appalling Street and my observations of activities and happenings at that mansion."

After sipping from a small glass of apple cider she continued, "I have been a close friend of Jane Olive Prudely since her birth in 1932. Since I am five years older than Jane I responded frequently during our early years to requests from her parents, Ovid and Samantha

Prudely, to come to their home and provide companionship and serve as a playmate for Jane Olive, their only daughter. Our friendship became close during the ensuing months and years as we shared our feelings, desires and fears."

Gladys moved about on her chair to restore comfort then added, "During the early years of Jane's life, Samantha became quite fascinated with the wild colors and patterns available on bolts of cloth available at local stores such as The E. Z. Nickel Emporium. She bought yards of such material and a new, expensive sewing machine. She became very adept at sewing as she created handkerchiefs, table runners and bed quilts. Samantha also fabricated all of Jane's clothes including her dresses and outer garments."

Frowning, Gladys reached for the glass of cider, sipped quietly then continued, "When Jane Olive approached her tenth birthday Samantha celebrated the upcoming event by continuing to dress her daughter in bright colors, decorated with, in my opinion, weird stick figures."

Gladys thought for a few seconds then continued, "Also, at times Samantha obtained large, empty flour sacks from people who had purchased flour from the Millsaap Flour Mill. She dyed these cotton sacks in garish colors. She cut the dyed material into long narrow strips, then sewed them together at the top to make outfits for Jane Olive. When Jane Olive walked about wearing those homemade dresses her movements seemed to make her body ebb and flow with shimmering ribbons and bits of fabric rippling and vibrating."

"Did Jane Olive resist or seem to be embarrassed when she wore the garish colored dresses?" asked Howie.

"No, she seemed to revel in being the object of her mother's attention."

Pausing to sip from her glass of cider, Gladys thought for a few seconds then added, "When I questioned Samantha about the rather bazaar dress patterns she replied, 'I'm following the trend enjoyed by my neighbors. They sew various materials together regardless of matching colors or patterns'."

"Did Samantha participate in any of the group 'sewing bees' or projects?" asked Howie.

"Yes, the neighbor ladies ordered patterns and fabric from firms advertising in leading magazines, such as *'Sewing Together'* and *'Sewing Trends'*. Evidently that fad of creating garish attire became quite popular with many women during the depression years of the 1930's."

During a very long pause the breathing of the cabinet members became very noticeable. Gladys inhaled deeply then continued, "During this period in the 1940's, Samantha became, and this description is my opinion, rather deranged and possibly paranoid. The outer garments she fabricated for Jane Olive consisted of strips of material depicting even more eccentric, wild and vivid patterns and colors. Samantha became withdrawn and reclusive. She remained inside the mansion for days on end."

Gladys hesitated and reached for the glass of cider, her hand trembling. As she lifted the glass it slipped from her hand and the liquid spilled across the table top and splashed on Inspector Snooper's shirt and trousers. He jumped up, fell backwards upsetting his chair.

Standing up and surveying his wet pants he quickly exited the room. A few minutes later everyone could hear the door to the bathroom at the rear of the jail slam shut.

Rather embarrassed, Gladys apologized and added, "Jane Olive refused to go outside the Prudely mansion attired in such outlandish dresses."

"How about Jane Olive's education?" asked Sam.

"She received some schooling from an aunt who came to the mansion three days a week."

"How many months or years did Samantha insist that her daughter wear such weird clothes?" asked Spade.

"Right up to the time of Jane Olive's death. She had just celebrated her tenth birthday by climbing the stairs to the top of the tower. She enjoyed looking through the telescope given to her by Ovid and Samantha a few years ago. Jane Olive told me the telescope gave her visual contact with the outside world, a rare event since Samantha required that Jane remain inside the mansion at all times."

Gladys inhaled deeply then continued. "Ovid and Samantha urged Jane Olive to celebrate her tenth birthday by sitting up in the dome of the tower and surveying the area at night. Her parents demanded she wear the special dress made from strands of colorful fabric cut out from flour sacks, a few dyed in bright colors and printed with hideous patterns depicting witches and the like on broomsticks."

"Do you know what caused Jane Olive's death?" asked the sheriff.

"Samantha told me her daughter died of a heart condition one night as she looked through the telescope. However, I never witnessed an ambulance arriving at the mansion. Shortly after Jane's death Ovid and Samantha both disappeared. I never saw them again."

"Spade, did you find evidence of heart failure when you examined The TatterBitty's corpse?" asked Sam.

"No, the death had occurred too many months prior to my examination for me to make any precise conclusions regarding the cause of death."

"If there are no further comments or questions we will adjourn for thirty minutes. Thank you for your comments today, Miss Fedders. We appreciate your time and candidness......Sam, please escort Gladys to the east door and to her car in our parking lot."

When Sam returned the sheriff stood up, stretched and loudly said, "Thank you all for your patience and willingness to hear the comments of Admiral Radar and Miss Gladys Fedders. The information they have shared is not only enlightening but also intriguing. Hopefully, we will soon be able to conclude our investigation of the activities and inhabitants of the Prudely mansion, including the tower."

After draining his glass of apple cider the sheriff added, "Now, I ask you to be patient and attentive for a few more minutes. Our resident mortician and member of this cabinet, Mr. Spade Digger, will share with us his opinions and conclusions regarding the corpse found stuffed in a large flour sack, and discovered by detectives Sam, Howie, and Inspector Snooper on the tower floor."

Spade jerked awake and sputtered, "Err, yes, if you don't mind I will refer to brief notes compiled by myself, medical collaborators and practitioners who examined the corpse found in the flour sack."

"Yes, yes, Spade, please proceed," ordered the sheriff, sighing, "Our backsides are very tired."

"The summary of opinions of the examining medical experts and myself state that the corpse is of a male dwarf. Cause of death is unknown and further inquiry as to the cause would be, in our opinion, unrewarding."

Spade coughed, loudly blew his nose, placed his hands against the small portion of his back, bent backwards, emitted a slight groan, then added, "Ovid, the assumed father and a possible agent of death, is dead. Samantha, the assumed mother and also a possible co-agent, is a patient at Polynurve Psychiatric Hospital, located at Mendtown, Indiana. It is possible that the birth of the dwarf caused self-imposed anguish and shame for the assumed parents. No one outside the Prudely household seems to know of the dwarf's birth or death. Hospital and county records yielded limited information."

Howie held up his hand and coughed. "Yes, detective," inquired the sheriff with impatience, "do you have an important question?"

"Yes, I would like to know if Spade has determined the name of the corpse we found in the flour sack, the person who is represented by the initals J. A. P., inscribed on the arm bracelet."

"We found one reference on a medical report naming the patient, Joseph Ashley Prudeley," responded Spade.

"Thanks, Spade, for your meticulous examination of the dwarf"'s corpse. At this point we will consider the death of the dwarf as natural.... Now, does any member have any further business to bring before this cabinet?"

Just as everyone breathed a collective sigh of relief anticipating the end of the stressful session, Sam stated, "Yes, Sheriff; Howie and I have just one more item that must be brought to the attention of the cabinet."

"Well, make it brief, Sam." ordered the sheriff, emitting a loud sigh and frowning.

"When Howie and I made the second visit to the tower for the purpose of finding evidence relevant to our cabinet members' discussion I stumbled against an old rusted laundry tub. Under that upset container we found this ten pound **M**illsaap flour sack with the highlighted letter **M** in the logo on the front."

Howie proceeded to remove the described flour sack from a wrinkled, paper grocery bag. He placed the sack on the conference table.

"Why do you bring this item to our attention, Sam? It appears just like all the sacks of flour you removed from the Prudely tower," commented the sheriff.

"Yes, that statement is true. However, when Howie and I thrust our hands into this sack of flour to examine the contents we found a scrap of paper."

Howie proceeded to untie the flour sack and empty the white contents on the conference table. Sam searched the flour with his fingers and produced a piece of weathered paper, smooth on two edges but with an irregular border on the third edge. He brushed the flour from the piece of paper with his handkerchief and placed it on a large, blank sheet of white paper he had brought to the cabinet session for the demonstration.

The members stood up, leaned over the table top and gawked at the paper, brownish with age especially along the edges. Upon closer examination the cabinet members agreed with Inspector Snooper, who had returned from the bathroom, bent over the table and declared, "That piece of paper is part of the map of this state of Indiana."

"Yeah," exclaimed Captain Firmly, "it's the southwest corner of the state map of Indiana, torn off, with a circle scribed in ink over some dot. Let me take a closer look. Yes, the circled dot is drawn around the name of a small town; it's the village of Pumpkin Blossom.....how odd."

"Let's not get too excited over a torn scrap of paper," suggested Sheriff Neverfine. "When folks travel by car they mark destinations, fuel stops and points of interest. That remnant of the map of Indiana probably ended up in a batch of wheat flour by someone's careless action or accident over at the Millsaap Flour Mill."

Then he added, "Perhaps a farmer-customer dropped the map segment in the customer waiting room at the flour mill. When the night workers found the scrap of map they discarded it by dropping it into the bin of flour to be bagged the next day."

With that statement the sheriff closed his note pad, stood up, walked to the refreshment table, grabbed two doughnuts and exited the conference room.

The remaining cabinet members stood up, speechless. They looked at each other, shrugged their shoulders and stepped toward the exit. Howie grabbed the torn, partial portion of the Indiana map, glanced at Sam and bent his head toward the door. The disarrayed pile of flour and the cotton sack remained on the conference table.

Soon, the only vestige of activity remaining in the room seemed to be a bevy of ants fighting over isolated bits of doughnuts scattered about on top of the refreshment table.

# *Chapter 17*

O N MONDAY EVENING OF THE next week, promptly at 6 o'clock,
Sheriff Neverfine greeted Snooper as the inspector entered
the jail through the east door to assume his duties on the night shift.
As they slowly shuffled together toward the sheriff's office the chief
law officer leaned over toward the Inspector and sternly informed,
"Snoop, the two men, Horst and Gerhard, apprehended recently at the
river near the Millsaap Flour Mill arrived today from the city holding
pen. They are being held in separate cells numbered 13 and 14, in the
male section. They will be our guests until their fate is decided by
the United States and German authorities."

"So the two former flour mill workers could be our prisoners for
some time."

"Yes, and I want you to keep a sharp eye on them. Maintain
a constant vigil. Observe their activities without seeming to be
intrusive. If either Gerhard or Horst cause us any trouble we will
move one of them to a distant cell."

"Thanks for the directive, Sheriff. I'll check on them every hour
or two."

"And tell the cook's helper, Zsofia, to be extra careful when she brings food to the prisoners. Perhaps you should accompany her and make sure all meals are properly and safely delivered to the prisoners......Remember the fate of Red Fox."

"You don't need to remind me about that event, Sheriff. Red Fox sure performed a graceful, acrobatic stunt when he fell to the floor and died while choking on Hungarian goulash."

"I'm on my way home, Inspector. Remember, keep a close eye on all our prisoners, especially Horst and Gerhard."

"Rest easy, Sheriff. When I am on duty everything is safe and secure."

A short time later the evening meal had been delivered on trays to the two prisoners by the cook, Zsofia, as the Inspector stood by. Horst looked at the food on his tray and gasped, "What is that stuff?"

Zsofia frowned and softly replied, "On your tray is an open-faced sandwich with wheat toast, butter, turo cheese and salami; a typical breakfast in Hungary."

When Horst opened his mouth to complain, Gerhard gruffly ordered, "Shut up, Horst. We haven't eaten since yesterday noon." Zsofia quietly retreated to the small jail kitchen. Snooper returned to the jail office.

After ten minutes of loud chewing and burping, Horst moved over closer to the steel bars that separated him from his cohort and murmered, "Gerhard, this food is worse than those stale sandwiches we stole from the corner general store down the street from The Millsaap Flour Mill."

"I agree, Horst. No food this insipid and gross would be served in our jails back home; and, I can speak from experience."

"Our pigs are blessed with more tasteful food than this slop," added Horst.

Thirty minutes later Zsofia returned with Inspector Snooper to retrieve the food trays. That night Gerhard continued with his vocal complaints. "When we napped at the flour mill the sacks of flour provided more comfort with fewer lumps than these threadbare mats that are supposed to be mattresses."

"Yah, that's true, Gerhard. And, that lawman on duty tonight who took our trays is the same officer who rowed the boat across the river with McWhimple. They call him Snooper. He seems to be as dense as the wood in an oak tree. He wouldn't be hired to clean jail toilets in Bavaria."

"You are so right, Horst. When he pointed his pistol at us down by the river his hand shook like he had the palsy."

"And his eyes had that wild look like some frightened animal."

"Gerhard, listen up. Since that dead-head is in charge here at the jail during the night-time hours maybe we can break out of here."

"Where would we go? We have no money or contacts here in Marston."

After a moment of thought Gerhard looked at Horst and added, "However, you are a proven expert at the art of relieving other persons of their money."

"That's true, but we need to escape from this dungeon first. Then in the morning perhaps I can spot a well-dressed man who would like to donate to our noble cause."

"Also, as we entered this jail I noticed several railroad tracks only two blocks away from this jail. After you increase our financial status we can jump on an empty box car and be in another state by tomorrow."

"Wait a minute, Gerhard. I just remembered something important."

"You do have a few good ideas, Horst. Let's have it."

"Do you remember the lenses we stuffed into marked sacks of flour at the Millsaap Flour Mill?"

"How could I forget those pieces of glass. The round lenses seemed to be the subject of most of the very pointed directions Red Fox gave us by sending signal light messages from the Prudely tower."

"And, Gerhard, you exposed your native artistic ability by using that artist brush with only two hairs to darken the right-hand leg of the letter M on the Millsaap logo."

"Thanks, Horst, for recognizing my artistic talent. I received excellent grades when I attended art classes at the reform school in Germany....You said you remembered something important. Did your pea-sized brain have another mini-explosion?"

"Gerhard, do you recall that night several months ago when Red Fox met us at the flour mill?"

"Not really; he talked with you because I utilized my break time by snoozing up in the cupola. That visit by Red Fox occurred a few days before his arrest by the local sheriff and this dopey lawman who is on duty at this jail tonight. I remember the next day you told me about his visit but you didn't mention any details. Get to the point, Horst, before the goofy Inspector makes his next rounds."

"Red Fox gave me a scrap of paper, a torn off section, perhaps a fourth, of the map of Indiana."

Horst hesitated then added, "He told me to hide the map section in a clearly marked bag of flour and take it to the Prudely tower. Red Fox said he would retrieve it later, follow the directions indicated on the map and locate a treasure hidden somewhere in the state of Indiana. Then Red Fox planned to escape from this country with the loot and head to South America."

"So we have a specific, marked bag of flour delivered as scheduled with other bags to the tower of the Prudely mansion. A scrap of paper, a section of the map of Indiana is hidden inside this sack of flour that now lies on the floor of the tower."

"You've got the idea, Gerhard. The bag is still there because Red Fox died before he could claim it."

"You are making my head spin, Horst. Why are you telling me this worthless information? We are prisoners and therefore not going to the tower in the Prudely mansion to recover any marked sack of flour."

Ignoring Gerhard's comment, Horst continued, "Red Fox informed me he placed a small black ink circle on a section of the map that marks a specific site. He said at that location secret instructions could be found to direct us to the second map section hidden at a different location in the state of Indiana."

"Now, Horst, I suppose you are going to tell me there are four scraps of paper, each a quarter section of the state of Indiana, leading us in sequence to some worthwhile horde of gold."

"You're right! That's exactly what Red Fox told me, Gerhard. Whoever locates and investigates the site indicated by black ink on the first map section will find the directions to the second location. When we locate the fourth site we will obtain the information that leads us to a tremendous trove of wealth."

"Horst, there are several problems with your sudden remembrance of that past episode and conversation involving Red Fox. First, since Red Fox came secretly at night a few weeks ago to the Millsaap Flour Mill and gave you this information, why didn't you wake me so I could be part of the conversation?"

"Because, Gerhard, your loud snoring up in the cupola told us that sleeping continued to be your priority. Also, we both know about your ugly frame of mind when you are awakened from your frequent naps during our breaks from work at the mill."

After another period of silence Gerhard, feeling left out, reached between the steel bars, punched Horst on the arm and asked another question. "Why did Red Fox choose to share this information with you, a lowly pawn who doesn't have the smarts to help him with that tour of the state of Indiana trying to locate an assumed treasure?"

"Red Fox expressed extreme anxiety that night. He couldn't sit still. I had never seen him so completely defeated, gloomy and unsure of his future. Before his exit he leaned over to me and confided, 'I am sure my arrest is imminent. I feel the jaws of American law enforcement tightening around my very throat'."

"Then he added, 'You and Gerhard are the only persons, my only remaining friends, who are free and able to follow the directions on the map of Indiana and locate the treasure'. Then, in a burst of optimism, he suggested if the three of us are ever reunited in The Fatherland or South America we can all benefit by sharing the newly-found wealth."

"Those comments by Red Fox are amazing, Horst. He at all times seemed so confident and sure of his capabilities. Why haven't you shared this information with me before today?"

"Because just before he left that night, Red Fox told me in explicit terms, 'Do not relate this conversation with anyone. If you do I will personally hunt you down and drive a railroad spike completely through your head'." Horst pointed to his head touching his right temple.

"And now that Red Fox is dead, you feel free to divulge his conversation with me. I can understand your logic, Horst. And I appreciate your confiding with me."

"We have always been honest with each other, Gerhard. Our survival through the years has depended upon our reliance upon each other and our frank conversations."

"Thanks, Horst, for trusting me with the secret conversation between you and Red Fox. However, we have two gigantic problems; one, we are cooped up in this miserable, dank jail; and two, even if we are able to escape from this 'slammer' the bag of flour containing the section of the map of Indiana we need is in the tower of the Prudely mansion."

"Yah, Gerhard, first we have to escape from this wretched jail. Then we can sneak through the alley and back streets to the Prudely mansion and tower. I placed a special mark on the bag of flour containing the first of four sections of that map of Indiana."

"And Horst, how do we proceed if the bag of flour containing the map is not in the tower at the Prudely mansion? Perhaps someone has cleaned the debris from the tower floor, including the sack of flour with a piece of the Indiana map."

"I remember a lot about that first map segment. It is the southwest part of the state of Indiana. And, the black circle is drawn around the location of that village of Pumpkin Blossom. Somewhere in that small village we will find the first direction to the location of the treasure."

Horst licked his lips, then continued, "We can go to Pumpkin Blossom and with your brains, Gerhard, we will discover the directions to the location of the second map section."

Gerhard, now energized, gazed at his partner through the steel bars separating their cells and smiled. "Now, I'm with you, Horst. Once again your brain cells have exploded and you have outlined a beautiful future for us. You are indeed a genius. We will make our way to Pumpkin Blossom and locate the directions to the second section of the Indiana map.....This is just like the mystery game, '**Search and Discover**'. I really enjoyed the challenge of that board game as a young lad in Germany."

"And, Gerhard, once we find the fourth section of the map and the treasure, we will have the resources to bribe our way back to our beloved Bavaria. No one will be able to stop us."

"You have done your share of planning for our future, Horst. While you whispered to me quietly relating your conversation with Red Fox, a plan developed in my mind. Now listen to me. When that imbecile of an Inspector makes his rounds tonight we will make our move. This is my plan of action for our escape. Lean over close to the steel bars that separate our abodes. I will share with you my brilliant scheme for our escape. Although the other prisoners are snoring and seem to be sound asleep we must be very discreet."

Horst pressed his face against the cold, steel bars, intent to hear every word. As he listened his frame became erect, his face stern and his eyes bright visualizing a resplendent future. He smiled.

Then Horst and Gerhard retired to their bunks hoping the next hours would pass quickly. As they lay fitfully their minds continued to anticipate the bold actions that would soon liberate them from the cold, steel bars standing as rigid sentries wrapping their cold forms around the prostate forms of two anxious desperate men.

# Chapter 18

INSPECTOR SNOOPER MADE HIS REGULAR hourly tour of the jail cells at midnight. He especially wanted to check on the activities of the men being held behind the bars in each cell. He breathed a sigh of relief as he noted only six prisoners occupied the cells tonight. No women had been placed behind bars for the past six weeks. As Snooper peered into each cell he noted all the prisoners seemed rather restless but dozing fitfully.

As he walked slowly past the cells holding Gerhard and Horst he noticed both men seemed to be asleep, their lips blubbering loudly with each breath exhaled. He quickly returned to the jail office, sank into Sheriff Neverfine's upholstered chair, placed his black boots on the floor under the desk, leaned back and closed his eyes.

Soon his dreams lifted him from the confines of the County Jail to his quaint home, a 1920's cottage the rooms decorated with striking, modern colors of paint, the walls adorned with framed pictures painted by his wife. Snooper smiled as his lovely wife, Mattie, appeared in his dream. His lips pursed.

Just as his puckered lips pressed against the full red lips of Mattie, his adorable wife, a loud bellowing yell punctured the peaceful jail atmosphere. The inspector bounced off his chair so fast his legs refused to support his thin frame. He fell rather awkwardly to the floor.

As he grabbed the edge of the huge wood desk for support and struggled upright a second series of wild screams resounded throughout the jail. The inspector sleepily grabbed his boots, forced them on the wrong feet and waddled awkwardly out of the office. He straightened his frame and raced toward the source of the shrill screaming. As he approached the area of the outbursts he found Gerhard prostate, squirming about on the concrete floor groaning and moaning.

When Gerhard glimpsed the presence of the inspector standing just outside his cell he clutched his prison shirt and yelled, "Help me! Please, somebody help me! My chest is exploding! I'm having a heart attack! Oh, woe is me!"

Horst, now standing, grabbed the steel bars at the front of his cell. Shaking the cold bars violently he demanded with a loud agonizing voice, "Help that man! If he dies in your jail you will be sued!"

Snooper quickly turned and ran to the jail office and dialed the telephone number for the medical doctor who had contracted with the county jail to assist prisoners who become ill while incarcerated. Within fifteen minutes Dr. T. Boner, dishevelled and clad in mismatched attire, met the inspector at the east door to the jail.

Snooper led the yawning doctor clutching his medical bag to Gerhard's cell and unlocked the door. Dr. T. Boner stepped into the cell, stooped over near the prisoner and loudly ordered, "Lie still so I can examine you!"

Just as Dr. Boner placed his medical bag on the floor Gerhard turned on his side and kicked the doctor violently on his ankles. As the doctor fell to the concrete floor, Gerhard jumped up and quickly immobilized a surprised Inspector Snooper with a 'hammerlock'.

Forcing Snooper up against the the steel bars he reached down and brusquely grabbed the keys attached to the inspector's belt. Yanking with force Gerhard now realized he not only possessed the keys to the jail cells but also the Inspector's belt. Snooper's trousers immediately fell to the floor.

Gerhard quickly exited the cell and slammed the door shut. Moving to the cell holding his partner he finally found the proper key and unlocked the door. Horst jumped out into the passageway and joined Gerhard. They glimpsed at the Inspector standing rather exposed and confined in the middle of Gerhard's cell. Snooper's chicken-like legs looked like frail, bent wheat straws connecting his boot tops and his shirt tail.

Horst and Gerhard both pointed at Snooper's legs and burst out in hilarious laughter as they romped toward the east door flailing their arms wildly. Horst jerked the door open and the duo burst out from the jail into the night air and freedom.

The good doctor, sitting on the floor of the cell and caressing his ankles, looked at Snooper's spindly, bowed legs, smiled and asked, "And you called me out of bed shortly after midnight for this?"

# Chapter 19

E ARLY THE NEXT MORNING THE sheriff barged through the east door to the jail and moved quickly to his office. Finding the space empty he looked toward the cells.

Hearing a faint call for help he ran in the direction of the pleading voice.

"Snoop," he bellowed, "what happened here last night? I found the east door wide open. You know I always keep that door securely locked."

"I have very bad news, Sheriff. The two prisoners, Gerhard and Horst, escaped last night. They tricked me into believing Gerhard had suffered a heart attack. I called Dr. T. Boner and when he arrived I accompanied him to Gerhard's cell. When the doctor stooped over and started to examine him, Gerhard rolled over and kicked the good doctor viciously on his ankle. When the doctor fell to the concrete floor Gerhard jumped up and grabbed my keys. He quickly stepped to the adjoining cell and released Horst. Then they left the doctor and me locked in the cell and they both fled out the east door."

"Snoop, the two prisoners must be miles away by now......and, where are your pants?"

"I completely lost my senses, Sheriff. I became very distraught. But don't worry. They can't get very far on foot."

"I'll call the Marston City Police Station and tell the captain about this jail break. Perhaps a city policeman cruising the streets can spot the two rascals....And, I repeat, where are your pants?"

"The ring holding all my keys is always attached to my belt. When Gerhard viciously grabbed my keys I lost not only the ring with the keys but also my belt. My trousers fell to the floor. The pants seemed to be soiled so I placed them in the laundry bag. I haven't have time to locate another pair of pants."

"Snoop, go home, freshen up and return at 1 0'clock. Captain Firmly has requested an emergency meeting of my cabinet for this afternoon."

"What seems to be on the captain's mind?"

"He would like for our group to review the recent statements given to our cabinet by Admiral Radar and Gladys Fedder."

"Thank you, Sheriff, for not asking any more embarrassing questions. I'll be back at 1 0'clock."

The sheriff, glancing at the Inspector's bowed, bird-like legs smiled widely as he suggested, "Snoop, you might want to wrap something around your legs so you won't be arrested for indecency."

Snoop frowned as he exited the east door and raced to his cruiser.

# Chapter 20

A T ONE O'CLOCK THAT AFTERNOON the jail conference room provided a pleasant gathering place for Sheriff Neverfine's cabinet members. Raucous laughter mixed with serious conversation dominated the atmosphere. Glazed doughnuts and steaming, aromic coffee rapidly disappeared from the refreshment table. Everyone, now seated, waited for the sheriff who would initiate the day's agenda.

At ten minutes past the hour the sheriff shuffled into the room, filled his coffee mug, grabbed one doughnut and stepped to his usual chair at the end of the conference table. Sitting down with a loud thump he apologized, "Sorry to be late; I just ended a disturbing telephone conversation with Captain Morsely at the Marston City Police Station."

He adjusted his ample frame to the cane bottom chair, then continued, "It seems that Gerhard and Horst, the two men who escaped from this jail last night," he paused to stare over his glasses at Inspector Snooper, "may have stolen a red pick-up truck from a Miss Mary Nupuls, a nurse at the local hospital. The captain told me a state policeman spotted a similar truck travelling south on Route 37 at a high rate of speed. The state cop could not pursue the speeding vehicle because he had just stopped a school teacher driving a red Mustang convertible at 80 miles per hour."

"Did Mary Nupuls give the Marston policeman a description of the men who stole her truck ?" asked Sam.

"Yes, it seems the two men stole her pick-up truck as she ended her night shift at the hospital. The nurse had walked to her truck and punched in the proper code. She had entered her truck and started the engine when one of the men, perhaps Gerhard, from her description, forced the door open and dragged her out of the truck and forced her to lie face down on the parking lot concrete."

The sheriff paused to drink from his coffee mug, then added, "Mary Nupuls returned to the hospital, called the Marston Police Station and reported the incident."

Howie immediately stood up and offered in a loud voice, "If Gerhard and Horst are the men who stole the nurse's truck we have a serious problem. They are surely a hundred miles away by now."

"Go ahead, Howie," suggested the sheriff, "why should we be involved? By now the suspects are probably out of our jurisdiction."

Captain Firmly spoke up and asked, "If the passengers in the speeding truck are Horst and Gerhard, why are the fugitives heading south?"

"Continue, Captain," proded Inspector Snooper, "what are your thoughts?"

"If we believe the two men are the German nationals, Horst and Gerhard, they are probably without passports or immigration papers.

To find the most logical place to escape from the United States they should be driving north toward the Canadian border where they might be able to sneak across at night."

"You have related a good point, Captain," remarked the sheriff. "Does anyone else have a comment or a suggestion as to how we should proceed?" asked the sheriff.

"I suggest we move on to the next item on your agenda, Sheriff," stated Captain Firmly. "No one seems to be able to verify the identity of the men in the truck stolen from the nurse. Probably a law enforcement agent in another county or town south of here will stop the vehicle and question the occupants."

"I agree," said Spade Digger, yawning, "no doubt an *All Points Bulletin* describing the incident and the escapees has been issued by the Indiana State Police.....some policeman south of here will pull the driver and the vehicle over and question the occupants of the truck."

"Alright, we'll move on to our second agenda item," stated the sheriff, shuffling a few papers. "But, I would suggest we haven't heard the last word about that red truck and the two escaped jail birds."

"Captain Firmly, do you have a question?"

"Yes, will Dr. McWhimple be questioned further by law enforcement officers here in Indiana or escorted back to Germany?"

"Since Dr. McWhimple has at times served as an agent responsible to Germany and the United States, his future is in the hands of government officials in both countries. Since he claims to be a citizen of the United States I would predict he will try to remain in this country."

Captain Firmly raised his hand and facing Sam and Howie, he asked, "As I recall our conversations and directives of a few weeks ago, Sheriff Neverfine asked you two detectives to investigate further the past operation of The Hireeze Employment Agency that operated out of the Prudely mansion. The members of this cabinet suspected the 'Agency' may have been involved in Human Trafficking. What findings resulted from your investigation?"

"Thank you, Captain for remembering that directive. Our inquiry led us to no conclusions. The contacts who seemed to be a possible source of information declined to share information."

"Therefore, is your inquiry closed?"

"Yes, at least until we locate another source of information."

"Well, we have been here for two hours," announced the sheriff. "We will meet again in two weeks, same time and place. This meeting is adjourned..... Sam and Howie please remain for a few minutes. I want to discuss a matter with you two detectives."

Five minutes later, after the cabinet members had shuffled out of the room, the sheriff, Sam and Howie sat at one end of the table.

"Sam and Howie," began the sheriff, "I regret your investigation regarding possible human trafficking during past years involving people at the Prudely mansion ended before you could collect pertinent data from people processed through The Hireze Employment Agency."

"Shall we initiate that investigation at a later time?" asked Howie.

"Perhaps; let's put that assignment on the shelf, at least temporarily.....Now, off the record, does your intuition suggest that we should be concerned about the escape of Horst and Gerhard, the two Millsaap Flour Mill workers?"

"Yes," answered Howie quickly. "Sam, share with the sheriff our recent conversation regarding the section of the Indiana map found in the sack of flour."

"Sheriff," began Sam, scooting forward on his chair and making eye contact, "Howie and I carefully examined and discussed for an hour the area displayed on the map segment. At first the map segment seemed to be a normal remnant that someone had torn off because the owner had some use for that particular map section."

"Yeah," interrupted Howie, "we thought it might have been used as a reference guide for an employed person who operates in that part of the state, such as a salesperson or a company representative for a travel agency."

"Then," stated Sam, "we used a magnifying glass to determine if we had missed some aspect on the map. Here, let me show you."

Retrieving a hand-held, round six-inch magnifying glass from his briefcase he stood up and held the magnifying glass a few inches above the map. "Sheriff, look through the glass and tell us if you see anything rather odd on this map."

The sheriff stood up, followed Sam's suggestion and adjusted the glass to his eyes. After a few seconds he responded, "No, I don't see anything strange. Wait a minute. Yes, yes, along a faint line representing a rural, county road, four very small letters are present, probably inscribed with an ink pen with a miniature point."

"What letters do you see, Sheriff?" enthused Sam.

"Let me adjust this glass just right....yes, the letters L-B-C-S are present along the line representing a road or route....but, what could those letters represent? And, why did someone spend time placing the letters on this torn section of an Indiana state map?"

"And, where does the road lead, Sheriff?" asked Howie.

"Why, it ends at Pumpkin Blossom, the dot on the map that is circled with black ink," responded the sheriff with interest.

"Also, Sheriff, notice the particles of white flour still remaining on the map, especially around the edges. Remember, Howie and I found this map section in a bag of flour hidden under a discarded laundry tub lying on the floor of the tower of the Prudely mansion."

"Yeah," spoke up Howie, "someone wrote the letters L-B-C-S on the map and placed it in the sack of flour."

"Your discovery, Sam and Howie, represents an intriguing mystery. Inspector Snooper and I are currently faced with too many concerns here at the jail and surrounding area to investigate these letters inscribed on the map of southwestern Indiana. Therefore, I am asking you two detectives to follow up and try to determine who inscribed these letters on this map and for what purpose."

"Also," continued the law officer, "determine the meaning for the letters L-B-C-S. Present your findings, if any, to our cabinet members at a future date of your choosing. Good luck and may God continue to keep you both safe."

The sheriff stood up, rubbed his backside, stretched and yawned. Without another word he exited the conference room. Sam and Howie looked at each other with raised eyebrows.

Finally, Sam picked up his briefcase, faced Howie and said, "I think those four letters L-B-C-S share a definite purpose, perhaps a directive for some intended observer."

"Yes, I agree. They are not intended for the casual traveler. But if the letters do have a special meaning for someone, who is that person?"

"I think we are headed for another adventure, Howie."

"You may be right. However, let's go home now and get reacquainted with our spouses. They will not be enthused about our return trip to southern Indiana."

# Epilogue

R ED FOX IS DEAD. HE no longer poses a threat to the law-abiding citizens of Marston. Byron Neverfine, sheriff of Gurant County inhales and breathes a sigh of relief. He can now concentrate on law enforcement issues affecting local citizens.

He remembers detectives Sam and Howie discovered German nationals Horst and Gerhard, two of Red Fox's patsies, had remained in Marston after the death of Red Fox. They had previously assisted the colonel with subversive activities during the recent war.

Using Morse Code they transmitted and received provocative messages while being employed on the night shift at The Millsaap Flour Mill located on the east bank of the Mississinewa River in that city.

Gerhard and Horst felt isolated and lost since the death of Red Fox. Without their mentor and protector their thoughts and daily movements were without purpose or direction.

During the war these furtive Morse Code messages, interpreted by cronies in the tower of the Prudely mansion, helped to facilitate the production and transfer of lenses for periscopes to be installed in

German submarines. Together with Dr. Nevin McWimple, a double undercover agent, Horst and Gerhard colluded as transfer agents in this illegal activity supplying the enemy with classified material. However, many of the lenses possessed an imperfection making them defective.

Now, three years after the war's end, who could be held responsible for receiving and transmitting these illicit and subversive messages at the tower? How about THE TATTERBITTY, the young girl dressed in outlandish clothing? Did she willingly participate in this clandestine activity? What would be her motive? Or did she act as a result of being coerced or threatened, and if so, by whom?

Perhaps detectives Sam and Howie, Sheriff Neverfine and the members of Sheriff Neverfine's cabinet will never know for certain the answers to these questions.

Certainly Horst and Gerhard sent and received many of these messages from the cupola on top of the flour mill. But where are these subversive agents now? They have not been seen since their daring escape from the local county jail when they duped Inspector Snooper and the local jail physician, Dr. T. Boner.

As Sheriff Neverfine and his colleagues ended their investigation of the illegal production and transfer of periscope lenses, a new enigma emerged. Found inside a sack of Millsaap flour hidden under a laundry tub on the floor of the mansion tower, Sam and Howie made an astounding discovery-a torn quarter- section of the the map of Indiana.

As they scrutinized this section of the map they noticed a circle of black ink had been inscribed around the dot representing the village of Pumpkin Blossom in southwestern Indiana.

What possible meaning can be derived from this captivating discovery? Why did the map section find a resting place in a sack of flour hidden under a laundry tub on the floor of the tower? Sheriff Neverfine is intrigued and assigns Howie and Sam the responsibility to determine if this recent discovery of the map section is a hoax or a serious breach of law.

Will the trip south to Pumpkin Blossom by Sam and Howie expose anything worthy of their extended time and effort? The complete episode could end quickly with the realization the two detectives have been duped by some unknown master of deception. However, the two detectives are determined to discover the presence of any illegal activity by conducting a thorough investigation.

The detectives are unaware that other persons are also intrigued by the inscription made by black ink on the Indiana map. Horst and Gerhard at this very moment are speeding south in a stolen red pick-up truck with avarice in mind. The two illegal residents also have knowledge about the map section with the inked inscription. They covet any trove of treasure supposedly hidden somewhere in Indiana. Their fervent hope is for the map section to lead them to a treasure. They hunger for these funds to finance their return to Bavaria.

Be sure to follow along as Sam and Howie are possibly thrust into a dangerous and thrilling adventure, the next captivating mystery in this series of escapades. You will want to follow this next adventure and participate with Sam and Howie as they match wits with dangerous and ruthless law breakers.